Grosset & Dunlap Edition 1971

Published pursuant to agreement with the
Hamlyn Publishing Group Ltd.

First published and © 1968 by The Hamlyn Publishing Group Ltd.

Library of Congress Catalog Card Number: 70-141635

Printed and Bound in Czechoslovakia by TSNP, Martin

ANIMAL FOLK TALES

By BARBARA KER WILSON
Illustrated by MIRKO HANAK

Grosset & Dunlap · Publishers · New York

CONTENTS

FIELD MOUSE AND
HOUSE MOUSE

A long time ago there was a Field Mouse who became acquainted with a House Mouse. The Field Mouse lived in the country; she had built herself a nest in a cornfield. The House Mouse lived in the town; her home was a hole in the wall.

One day the Field Mouse invited the House Mouse to dine with her in the country.

"I should simply love to dine with you, dear friend," gushed the House Mouse.

"Good," said the Field Mouse.

But when the House Mouse arrived at the nest in the cornfield, she discovered that there were only barley ears and corn stalks for dinner.

She turned up her pink nose. "This is very frugal fare," she said disdainfully. "I am not used to such plain food. Why, my friend, you live like an ant! Let's go back to my place and have dinner there instead. I have all sorts of good things to eat at home. We shall have a feast, I promise you!"

"Just as you like," said the Field Mouse.

So off they went to the town. The Field Mouse soon discovered that the House Mouse had not been idly boasting. Her friend led her into a room where there was a table laden with all sorts of good things to eat. The Field Mouse had never seen so much food! There was a loaf of crusty white bread, a ripe yellow cheese, a jar of golden honey, a platter of sweet dates, and a dish piled with luscious grapes, oranges, figs, and rosy apples.

"This is a feast, indeed!" squeaked the Field Mouse in astonishment. "I did not realize you lived in such luxury, my dear. I am ashamed to think I offered you such wretched hospitality back home in the cornfield."

The House Mouse smirked. "Help yourself, my dear," she said proudly.

The Field Mouse had just dipped her whiskers into the jar of golden honey when there was a sound of approaching footsteps, and the door of the room was suddenly flung open.

"Quick, into the wall!" squeaked

8

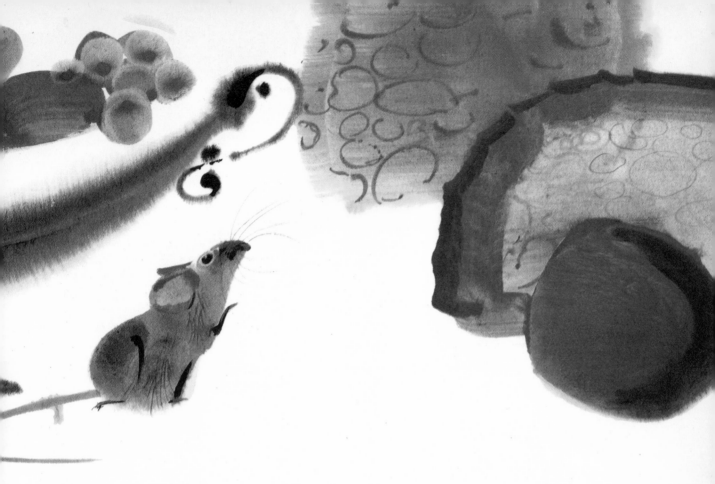

the House Mouse in alarm — and they both scuttled out of sight through the hole.

After a few moments the person who had entered the room went out again, and the two Mice dared to come out from their hole.

"Now we can start our meal again," said the House Mouse. "I must apologize for that interruption. Do go ahead, please — I'm sure you must be as hungry as I am."

The Field Mouse perched on the cheese and began nibbling at the rind. Alas! She had just savored the first delicious mouthful when once more the sound of approaching footsteps was heard, and the door of the room was flung open a second time.

Again the two Mice jumped from the table and ran to take cover in the wall.

"Oh, my dear friend," groaned the Field Mouse, quaking with fear, "I really must bid you good-by. I cannot take any more of this sort of thing. My nerves and digestion will not stand it! You may eat as much as you like of all those good things on the table. But I would rather gnaw my

own barley ears and corn stalks in peace, without having to watch out all the time, in case someone discovers me. A life of luxury is not for me!"

And she returned to her nest in the cornfield, and enjoyed a late supper.

THE GOAT, THE RAVEN, THE RAT AND THE TORTOISE

In the dark green jungle, where monkeys chatter in the treetops and snakes slither through the grass, and the Hunter comes silently with his net and spear, a little white Goat came to a water hole. But she was afraid to put down her head to drink.

Now there were three other creatures beside the water hole: a glossy black Raven, perched in a tree; a bright-eyed Rat, looking out from his hole in the bank; and a Tortoise who lurked beneath the water.

All three saw that the little Goat was afraid to drink, and they wanted to help her. The Raven looked down and all round from his lofty perch, and called out to the Tortoise: "There is no enemy in sight. Tell the little Goat that it is safe for her to drink."

So the Tortoise poked his head above the water and told the Goat that she might quench her thirst without fear. Then the bright-eyed Rat crept from his hole and asked the Goat why she had been afraid to drink.

"I have just escaped from the Hunter," she replied, "and I feared lest he should come up behind me and trap me in his net while I was drinking."

Then the Tortoise said: "You see that the Raven, the Rat, and myself are good friends. Why do you not join our company? It is better than living in the jungle alone."

The Goat gladly agreed to join their company, and for a while the four creatures lived happily together.

But one day, the little white Goat was nowhere to be found.

"I fear that something has happened to her," the Raven said sadly.

"Perhaps she has met the Hunter," said the Rat.

"We must try to find her," said the Tortoise.

The Raven spread his glossy black wings and flew high above the treetops, looking everywhere for the little white Goat. At last he spied something far below on the ground, and when he came down to earth he found the Goat caught fast in the Hunter's net.

"Help me!" cried the Goat. "The Hunter has left me in his net while he goes off to trap other animals. When he returns, he will kill me."

The Raven was distressed to see the Goat in such a predicament. "I will fly back to the others and ask them what we should do to help you."

He returned to the water hole and told the Rat and the Tortoise what had happened to the Goat.

"Our friend Rat could gnaw through the meshes of the Hunter's net," said the Tortoise.

"What a good idea!" said the Rat. "The Raven can carry me in his bill and his claws to the place where the Goat is trapped."

So off flew the Raven with the Rat dangling from his bill and his claws. The little Goat was overjoyed to see her friends, and the Rat set to work to bite through the Hunter's net with his sharp teeth. He had just completed his task when along came the Tortoise.

The Raven, the Rat, and the Goat were dismayed to see him.

"Alas!" cried the Goat. "Soon the Hunter will return, and how will you escape from him, friend Tortoise? The Raven can fly into the tall trees; the Rat can creep into a hole in the ground; I can run swiftly away. But you can only crawl slowly, slowly along the ground. You will never escape from him."

At that moment, they heard the stealthy tread of the Hunter coming through the jungle. The Raven flew to the top of a tree; the Rat crept into a hole; and the Goat ran swiftly away. But all the poor Tortoise could do was to crawl slowly, slowly towards a clump of grass.

The Hunter was very angry when he saw his torn net and realized that the Goat had escaped. He looked round, and immediately spotted the Tortoise.

"Ha! A plump Tortoise is better than nothing!" he cried. And he seized the Tortoise, put him in a sack, and strode off.

The Rat peeped out from his hole and saw what had happened. He told the Raven and the Goat.

"Now we must rescue the Tortoise," said the Raven.

"How shall we do it?" said the Rat.

"Let me run before the Hunter," suggested the Goat. "Then he will drop the sack to chase me, and the Rat can release the Tortoise."

The Raven and the Rat agreed to this plan, and the Goat set off. Soon the Hunter caught sight of her as she ran before him through the jungle. He dropped his sack and began to chase her.

Quickly the Rat ran to the sack and bit through the string that tied it. The Tortoise crawled out thankfully.

Meanwhile, the Goat led the Hunter such a dance that at last he lost track of her altogether. He decided he had had enough hunting for one day, and returned to the place where he had left his sack. "At least I have a fine plump Tortoise here," he thought.

When he found the empty sack, he could scarcely believe his eyes.

"First the fleet-footed Goat escapes me, and then the slow-moving Tortoise!" he cried.

As for the Goat, the Raven, the Rat, and the Tortoise, they vowed always to help one another in trouble, and in this way they lived in safety in the jungle for many years.

THE
SWIMMING RACE

Once upon a time, in a far-off land where
the sun shines all day long, there were two
Tortoises who were twins. They were so
alike that you could not tell one Tortoise
from the other. One fine day, the first
Tortoise said to his brother: "Let us play a
trick upon the great gray Hippopotamus
who wallows in the mud of the river. Let
us challenge him to a swimming race!"

"But we could not win such a race,"
protested the second Tortoise. "The Hippopotamus can swim much faster than we
can."

The first Tortoise smiled a sly smile.
"Ah, brother, you have not heard my plan.
Listen!" And he whispered in the second
Tortoise's ear.

When the second Tortoise heard his
brother's plan, he too smiled a sly smile.
Then they set off together for the river,
where the great gray Hippopotamus was
wallowing in the mud. The first Tortoise
approached the Hippopotamus by himself, while the second Tortoise swam
quietly to the opposite bank of the river.

"Ho, Hippopotamus! Ha, Hippopotamus!" shouted the first Tortoise. "I
challenge you to a swimming race!"

The great gray Hippopotamus shook
with laughter when he heard the Tortoise's challenge. "Go away, you foolish
little Tortoise!" he cried. "You could
never swim as fast as me!"

But the Tortoise challenged him again.
"I will race you to the opposite bank, and
back again!" he said.

"Very well," agreed the Hippopotamus at last.

"There is only one condition I want to make," the Tortoise told him. "And that is that we must swim under the water all the way."

The Hippopotamus agreed to this, too, and so the race began. The Hippopotamus was such a powerful swimmer that he reached the opposite bank in the blink of a crocodile's eye. Imagine his astonishment when he found the Tortoise there before him, sitting high and dry on the bank! *He* was not to know it was not the same Tortoise, but his twin brother!

"Ho, Hippopotamus! Ha, Hippopotamus! What a slowpoke you are!" cried the second Tortoise. "I've been waiting for you."

"This is ridiculous!" spluttered the Hippopotamus. "No Tortoise can swim faster than me! Let us swim back again – I'll soon show you who will win the race this time!"

"Very well," agreed the second Tortoise; and he jumped into the water.

The great gray Hippopotamus turned round and moved even faster beneath the water than before. This time he reached the opposite bank in half a blink of a crocodile's eye.

What do you think he found? There was the Tortoise, sitting high and dry on the bank as before! *He* was not to know it was not the same Tortoise, but his twin brother!

"Ho, Hippopotamus! Ha, Hippopotamus! I see you are too slow for me!" the first Tortoise called mockingly. "I shall have to challenge someone who can swim really fast next time I want to hold a race!"

The great gray Hippopotamus could only splutter indignantly. Sadly he went back to wallow in the mud, wondering and wondering how a Tortoise could possibly swim faster than he could.

As for the twin Tortoises, they laughed and laughed over the clever trick they had played.

THE HORSE AND
THE FOX

The Horse had grown old in the service of his master, and he was no longer able to perform a full day's work. He could not spend all day in the fields harnessed to the plow, nor pull the loaded farm cart to market each week. His master was a hard man; since the faithful Horse could not carry out his duties, he refused to give him food and shelter. He turned the Horse out of the stable, saying:

"There is no place here for creatures who do not earn their keep, so take yourself off, and don't let me see you again!" Then he added: "You may come back to live in my stable and eat my oats if you can show yourself to be as strong as a lion!" And he burst into roars of mocking laughter.

The poor old Horse wandered across the countryside. His head drooped and he felt very sorry for himself. At last he reached the great forest where the wild beasts lived. Here he met the red-brown Fox.

"Why do you hang your head so miserably?" the Fox asked the Horse.

The Horse sighed. "I can no longer work for my master, and so he has turned me out to fend for myself. He has forgotten the years of faithful service I have rendered him."

"Alas!" said the Fox. "Men are cruel creatures. Did he not give you a chance to stay?"

The Horse recalled his master's parting jibe. "He told me I might return to the stable if I could prove myself as strong as a lion. But that is impossible. I am old and feeble."

The Fox turned his head on one side and considered the problem. Then he said: "Do as I say and all will be well. Just stretch yourself out stiffly on the ground

as if you were dead, and don't move. I will return."

The Horse did as he was told, and lay on the ground. Meanwhile, the Fox trotted off to the Lion's den in the forest.

"Lord Lion," he said, bowing low, "there is a dead horse lying on the ground a little distance away. Follow me, and you shall enjoy a feast."

The Lion got up eagerly and followed the Fox, who led him to the place where the Horse lay. How the Horse trembled inside when he heard the Lion prowling round his body! But still he made no movement, and lay still, for he trusted the red-brown Fox.

Then the Fox said: "It is not fitting that you should enjoy your feast in such a public place, Lord Lion. Allow me to fasten the Horse to you by his tail; then you can drag him into your den and eat him there."

The Lion was glad to do as the Fox suggested; and he lay down so that the Fox might tie the Horse to him. But now the crafty Fox showed his cunning. He twisted the Horse's tail so tightly round the Lion's legs that nothing could break the bond.

"Now pull, old Horse, pull as hard as you can!" he cried.

The Horse got to his feet and began to pull, and so he dragged the mighty, helpless Lion along behind him. The Lion roared and struggled, but he could not break the knots the Fox had made. In this manner the Horse drew the Lion out of the forest and across the fields, all the way back to his master's farm. You can imagine how amazed his master was to see his old Horse arrive at the stable door towing a Lion behind him.

"So, my old Dobbin, you have proved yourself *stronger* than a Lion!" he cried. "That is one better than the task I set you! Very well: you may return to your place in the stable, and I will feed you and look after you, even though your working days are over."

He kept his word, and the Horse spent the rest of his life in comfortable idleness.

15

HALF-CHICK

In the sunny land of Spain, where oranges grow on trees, a black Hen sat upon the egg she had laid, and waited for her chicken to hatch out. Presently she heard a *tap-tap-tapping,* and at last the chicken broke through the shell. But what a funny little chicken he was! The mother Hen squawked in astonishment when she saw him. For he was only half a chicken! He hopped out of the broken egg on his one leg, and waggled his one yellow wing, and looked up at his mother with his one bright eye. However, the black Hen loved her little Half-Chick every bit as much as his brothers and sisters, who were just ordinary chickens. As Half-Chick grew up, he proved to be as mischievous as two whole chickens put together! He was always in trouble from some prank or other. He teased the great Dog that guarded the farmyard, was rude to the fine Rooster, and ran squawking behind the proud gray Geese as they waddled down to the stream.

Then one fine day, Half-Chick came hopping up to the black Hen and said: "I am bored with living here in this dull farmyard. I am off to Madrid to seek my fortune."

How the Black Hen clucked when she heard this news! Madrid, the capital of Spain, was many miles away.

"Why do you want to go to Madrid?" she asked.

"I want to see the King of Spain," replied Half-Chick. "And I am sure the King of Spain will be pleased to see *me,*" he added.

"Madrid is a very long way from here," the black Hen warned him. "It is better to stay at home in the farmyard."

"I'll get there!" Half-Chick assured her.

And off he started, hop-hop-hop, on his journey to the great city. Quite soon he came to a little Brook. The Brook was in a sad state. Its water was choked with green weeds.

"Help me, little Half-Chick!" gurgled the Brook. "Drag away these green weeds, so that I may run freely once more."

But Half-Chick did not want to help the Brook. "I can't stop now," he cried. "I'm off to Madrid to see the King of Spain." And he went on his way.

Now he came to a dark wood, and in a clearing he saw a fire that the woodcutters had lit. The fire was dying for lack of fuel.

"Help me, little Half-Chick!" crackled

the Fire. "Fetch a few sticks and throw them on me, so that I can burn brightly again."

But Half-Chick did not want to help the Fire. "I'm in a hurry," he cried. "I'm off to Madrid to see the King of Spain." And he went on his way.

He hopped along for many miles, and at last he reached the great city of Madrid. Tall buildings towered on either side of the cobbled streets, which were thronged with people. Little Half-Chick hopped on until he came to the royal palace. A flowering chestnut tree grew by the gateway to the palace. Its five-fingered leaves and pink candles tossed to and fro, and from the branches of the tree Half-Chick heard the voice of the Wind calling to him.

"Help me, little Half-Chick!" moaned the Wind. "I am tangled in this tree. Please set me free!"

But Half-Chick did not want to help the Wind. "I have no time to listen to you!" he cried. "I have come to see the King!"

He crossed the palace courtyard, where soldiers in shining silver armor stood guard. Then he saw an open door. In another moment he had hopped through the doorway and found himself in a lofty room. A huge fire burned, and a spit with roasting meat was slowly being turned by two servants. In the middle of the room was a table loaded with pots and pans and dishes. It was the royal kitchen.

Half-Chick did not know this, however. "What a grand apartment!" he thought. "This must be the King's throne-room!"

Just then a man wearing a white apron and a tall white pleated hat came into the kitchen. He was the royal cook.

Half-Chick did not know this, however. "Here is the King of Spain himself!" he thought. "So that's what the royal crown looks like!"

And he stood up very straight on his one leg, and saluted the cook with his one yellow wing.

The cook looked down at Half-Chick and remarked cheerfully: "Chicken broth for dinner today! You are the very fellow I was looking for!"

And he seized the unlucky Half-Chick in his hands, and threw him, feathers and all, into a big iron pot that was bubbling on the fire.

"Oh, Water!" squeaked Half-Chick, "how you are scalding me!"

"Have you forgotten the Brook choked with green weeds, and how you refused to help it?" asked the water. And it went on bubbling.

Next, Half-Chick appealed to the Fire.

"Oh, Fire!" he squeaked, "how your flames are burning me!"

"Have you forgotten our meeting in the wood, and how you refused to fetch a handful of sticks to throw on me?" asked the Fire. And it went on burning.

Then Half-Chick heard a whistling sound in the kitchen chimney, and he called out in despair: "Oh Wind! Put out the fire and overturn the pot, so that I may escape from this dreadful fate!"

"You did not help me when I was tangled in the chestnut tree," whistled the Wind. "Nevertheless, I will take pity on you."

And the Wind blew and whipped Half-Chick up out of the cooking-pot, up, up the dark sooty chimney, up, up, up over the roofs of Madrid.

"Stop! Stop!" cried Half-Chick.

But the Wind did not stop until it had blown little Half-Chick right on top of the steeple of the highest church in Madrid, so high that it touched the clouds in the sky.

"There you are," said the Wind.

And there the Half-Chick remains to this day! He is gilded now with gold paint, and the sun glints on his splendor. Often the townsfolk far below hear a creaking sound, and they look up to the steeple and say: "What a noise the weather-cock is making today!" They do not know that the creaking sound is really the Half-Chick repeating sadly to himself over and over again: "I wish I had listened to my mother's advice, and stayed at home in the farmyard!"

THE JELLYFISH AND THE MONKEY

In the dim, dark world of the sea, long ago, Rin-Jin the Sea King took a young and beautiful Dragon for his wife. But they had only been married a little while when the Dragon Queen fell ill. Rin-Jin sought the advice of the Cuttlefish, whose fame as a physician was known throughout the sea. But even the clever Cuttlefish could not tell how the Queen might get well again.

"There is no cure for this illness," he said, shaking his head. "The Queen will soon be dead."

When she heard these words, the Queen sobbed and cried. "No," she said, "there is one thing that will cure me! I will recover immediately if I eat the liver of a monkey. Please bring me a monkey's liver if you want to save my life!"

"It shall be done, my love," said Rin-Jin.

So the Sea King summoned a Jellyfish to come before him. At that time, the Jellyfish did not look as he does now. He had a hard, thick shell.

"Jellyfish," said the King, "I have a most important task for you to perform. I want you to swim to the land and return with a monkey on your back. The Queen must eat his liver if she is to be cured of her illness. You just use all your cunning to persuade the Monkey to come here with you. Tell him about all the wonders of our dim, dark world. But don't return without him, or it will be the worse for you!"

The Sea King sounded very stern as he spoke these words, and the Jellyfish wobbled with fright inside his shell. "I won't fail your Majesty!" he promised.

The Jellyfish set off on his mission. He swam up to the surface of the sea, and soon reached the shore. A little way inland, he came to a pine tree. And sitting on a branch of the pine tree, what should he see but the very creature he was looking for – a Monkey!

18

"Good-day, Monkey!" he called. "What a dull and miserable life you must lead in this place, to be sure! I have just come from the wonderful world of the sea, which is ruled by Rin-Jin, the great Sea King. Oh, you can't imagine how beautiful it is! There are delicate coral reefs, and colored seaweeds, and all manner of fruits and plants that are good to eat. The flowers and trees that grow here on the land are nothing compared with those that thrive in the sea!"

The Monkey was most interested to hear what the Jellyfish had to say. He, too, wanted to see this wonderful kingdom of the sea.

"I tell you what," said the Jellyfish, "I will take you there if you like. Jump on my back, and we'll set off at once."

"I should like that very much," said the Monkey. He got down from his tree and settled himself on the Jellyfish's shell.

Off they went through the sea, down to the dim, dark world of the great Sea King. When they were about halfway there, the Jellyfish suddenly thought of something.

"By the way, Monkey," he said, "I suppose you have got your liver with you, haven't you?"

"What a strange question to ask me!" said the Monkey suspiciously. "Why do you want to know?"

Then the foolish Jellyfish told him: "Our beloved Sea Queen is very ill, and she will not get well unless she eats a monkey's liver. As soon as we arrive, the Cuttlefish will take your liver, the Queen will eat it, and so she will be restored to health."

"So that's it!" exclaimed the Monkey. "I wish you had told me this before we set out!"

"But then," said the Jellyfish, "I doubt if you would have agreed to come with me."

"My dear fellow," protested the Monkey, "you're quite mistaken! I should have been just as delighted to accompany you. It so happens that I have several spare livers hanging in that very pine tree where you found me, and of course I would gladly spare one to save the life of the Sea Queen. What is one liver when a life is at stake? But the thing is that all my livers are in that tree; I don't happen to have one with me. This is most unfortunate – you will have to take me back to the land so that I can get one for you."

No sooner had the sly Monkey said this than the believing Jellyfish turned round and swam back to the land. When they reached the pine tree, the Monkey sprang up into the topmost branches.

"You stupid old Jellyfish!" he cried. "You'll never have my liver unless you catch me first!" And he danced with glee.

Sadly the Jellyfish went back to the sea once more.

When he came to the palace of Rin-Jin and told him what had happened, the King fell into a great rage. The Jellyfish trembled with fright, as well he might, for the King cried: "Beat this fellow to a jelly! Beat him until he hasn't a bone left in his body!"

And that was how the Jellyfish lost his shell.

THE CONCEITED SPIDER

Big black furry Spider had a very good opinion of himself. He lived long ago in Africa, where all the stories and legends that men and animals told one another were about a Great Being called Nyankupon. Most of the animals and men were quite happy with this arrangement, for they realized that none of them were as great or worthy of high honor as Nyankupon. But one day Spider said to himself:

"Why should all the stories and legends be about stupid old Nyankupon? Why shouldn't some of them be about ME?"

And off he went to see the Great Being called Nyankupon.

"What do you want with me, you black furry creature?" Nyankupon asked Spider.

"I have come to ask that in future some of the stories and legends that men and animals tell to one another should be about ME," Spider said boldly.

Nyankupon smiled a wise smile. "I will grant your request on condition that you bring me three things," he told Spider. "The first is a jar full of bees; the second, a boa constrictor; the third, a fierce tiger."

"I will do that," Spider promised him.

Off went Spider to fulfill the first of his three tasks. He took a clay pot and went to a place in the forest where he knew the bees gathered nectar. Sure enough, there was a great swarm of bees humming and buzzing as they worked busily. Spider waved the clay pot in the air and said: "Listen, bees! Nyankupon the Great Being and I have had an argument. Nyankupon says that you would not be able to fly into this clay pot. I say you could. Which of us is right?"

"Of course we could! Of course we could!" the bees hummed loudly, and just to prove it they flew into the mouth of the pot.

Cunning Spider waited until the pot was quite filled with bees, then he sealed it up and took it to Nyankupon. "Here is your jar full of bees, Nyankupon," he said.

Nyankupon was very surprised that Spider should have succeeded in carrying out the first of his tasks so quickly. "Now you must bring me the boa constrictor," he told him.

"I will do that," Spider promised him.

He took a long stick and a strong vine, and went off to a place in the forest where he knew a boa constrictor lived.

"Listen, boa constrictor!" he cried. "Nyankupon the Great Being and I have had an argument. Nyankupon says you are not as long as this stick. I say you are. Which of us is right?"

"The only way to settle the argument is to measure my length against the stick," said the boa constrictor; and he laid himself out straight from end to end of it.

At once Spider took his strong vine and tied the boa constrictor securely to the stick. Then he carried him off to Nyankupon.

"Here is your boa constrictor, Nyankupon," he said.

Nyankupon was amazed when he saw that Spider had completed the second of his three tasks. "Now you must bring me the fierce tiger," he told him.

"I will do that," Spider promised him.

This time, Spider thought of an even more clever plan. Before he set out, he took a needle and thread and sewed up his right eye. Then off he went to the den where he knew a fierce tiger lived. As he drew near the den, he began to sing a happy song. The tiger heard his song, and came out to see what was happening.

"What makes you sing so happily?" he asked Spider.

"Why, don't you see that my right eye is sewn up?" Spider replied. "I can see such wonderful things with it that I must sing about them."

The tiger was very curious. "Please sew up my eye," he begged Spider. "No – sew up *both* of my eyes, and then I'll be able to see twice as many wonderful things as you!"

Spider lost no time in sewing up the tiger's two eyes with his needle and thread. And then, having made the tiger blind and helpless, he led him to Nyankupon.

"Here is your fierce tiger, Nyankupon," he said.

Nyankupon was astounded when he realized that Spider had carried out his third task. "O Spider, I see that you are indeed a clever creature," he said, "and from this day forward, men and animals shall tell one another stories and legends of Anansi the Spider."

It happened just as Nyankupon the Great Being decreed. From that day forward, men and animals began to tell of Anansi the Spider – and that was the first of the stories they told one another.

THE SNAIL, THE ANT AND THE SHRIMP

Long, long ago, when the world was young, a Snail, an Ant, and a Shrimp agreed to cultivate a rice field together. But before the story continues, you must first understand that in those far-off days, these three creatures looked very different from the way they do now. The Snail was completely hidden inside his shell; he never came out of it at all. The Shrimp was a colorless creature. And the Ant had a plump, sausage-shaped body.

The three friends discussed how they ought to spend their days.

"We must divide the work equally," said the Snail.

"No one must work harder than anyone else," agreed the Ant.

"I think it would be best if you two were to labor in the field while I look after our house and do the cooking," said the Shrimp.

So it was arranged; the Shrimp was to stay at home while the Snail and the Ant went out to the rice field.

The next morning, the Snail and the Ant set out at daybreak, taking with them some food that the Shrimp had prepared. It was so early that the birds had not yet flown away from the trees. The Snail and the Ant worked hard all day long, cutting the green rice in the field. By the time the sun began to set, they felt ready for a really good meal.

Meanwhile, back in their house, the Shrimp was very busy preparing dinner. He had been to the forest to collect some firewood and a bunch of young beets and now he stood stirring a pot of beet soup over the fire. He tried a spoonful to see how it tasted.

Delicious!

At that moment, he heard his two friends returning from the rice field. Quickly he removed the pot of soup from the fire. But alas! In his haste, he fell head-over-heels into the simmering liquid.

"Help! Help!" cried the poor Shrimp. "Snail, please help me!"

"Just a minute!" answered the Snail, "I must first blow my nose."

But alas! The Snail blew his nose so hard that he fell half out of his shell. "Help! Help!" he shrieked. "Ant, please help me!"

"Just a minute!" the Ant replied, "I must first tighten the belt around my waist."

But alas! The Ant pulled the belt so tightly that she divided her body almost in two.

So the three friends all met with a terrible fate; and to this day, you will find that the Shrimp is boiled bright red; the Snail lives half out of his shell; and the Ant's body is divided almost in two.

THE FOX OUTWITS
THE LION

There was once an old Lion who had grown too weak to hunt his prey. He could no longer chase the running Deer, or fight the wild Boar. He only had strength enough to lie in the sun and watch the world go by. And he had only his wits and wisdom left to help him get his food.

He lay down in a cave, pretending to be ill. Whenever any animal was foolish enough to visit him, he would seize and devour it as soon as it came within reach.

One day a Fox passed by the cave. He saw the old Lion lying at the entrance, with his head resting on his paws, but being a crafty creature, the Fox kept his distance.

"How goes it with you, Lord Lion?" the Fox inquired.

The Lion slowly raised his head. "Badly," he answered in a feeble voice.

"I fear I am not long for this world."

"I am sorry to hear that," said the Fox.

But still he did not move nearer to the cave.

"I am so ill that I can hardly hear what you are saying, my friend," the Lion went on. "Will you not come into my cave and talk with me?"

The Fox looked carefully at the sandy earth around the cave, and then he shook his head.

"I fear I cannot accept your invitation, Lord Lion," he replied. "For I see the tracks of many animals going into your cave, but none coming out again! I do not wish to share their fate!"

With this the Fox vanished into the trees, and the Lion growled with disappointment. The Fox was the only animal clever enough to recognize the danger that lurked within his cave.

THE FOX TRICKS
THE WOLF

It was spring. In the forest the trees were putting out fresh green leaves, and the birds nested in their branches. A hungry Wolf came stalking like a lean gray shadow through the forest. Presently he met a red-brown Fox who was busy eating a fine plump hen.

"Give me half of that hen," begged the Wolf. "I am starving."

The Fox did not want to share the hen with the Wolf. He looked up with a crafty gleam in his eye.

"I will do better than that," he said. "There are plenty more fine plump hens where this one came from. Follow me and I will show you."

The Wolf followed the Fox, who led him out of the forest, across a field, and into a farmyard. He stopped by the door of a henhouse.

"Just go in there, my friend," he told the Wolf, "and you will find a feast of your own for the taking."

The Wolf did as the Fox directed. He went inside the henhouse, and saw a row of fine plump hens perched there.

"Here is a feast, indeed!" he said to himself. He was just about to pounce on the finest and plumpest hen of all when –

"*Cock-a-doodle-do!* A thief in the hen-house! *Cock-a-doodle-do!*" It was the Cock that crowed, strutting up and down and flapping his wings in the Wolf's face.

The Wolf was very frightened. He knew the noise would wake the farmer. He turned round and ran to the door of the henhouse – only to find that the Fox had fastened it from the outside! And now the farmer came running across the yard with a thick stick in his hand.

"I'll teach you to steal my fine plump hens!" he cried when he found the Wolf in the henhouse. "Take that – and that – and that!" And he beat the Wolf with his stick.

The Wolf howled with pain and loped away covered with bruises – a sorry sight. He vowed he would get even with the Fox for treating him so shabbily. "Just wait till we meet again, Mister Fox!" he snarled.

It was summer when the Wolf met the Fox for the second time. The sun shone from the blue sky, and the meadows were filled with flowers. The Wolf came upon the Fox licking out a butter churn by the roadside.

"That was a shabby trick you played on me when you locked me in the henhouse," the Wolf told him. "Now you can just give me some of that butter by way of making amends."

The Fox pretended to be very sorry. "I hope your bruises were not too painful, friend," he said. "I would like to give you some of this butter, but I fear that is impossible, because I have just finished the very last morsel." He licked his lips as he spoke. "However, it is quite a simple matter to enjoy a feast of butter. All you have to do is to lie down in the road as if you were dead. By and by a peasant will come along in his cart, taking his churns of butter to market. When he sees you – a dead wolf lying in the road – he will want to sell your skin at the market, and will put you in his cart, along with all the butter. Then all you have to do is to eat as much butter as you like, and when you have finished, jump off the cart!"

The Wolf thought this an excellent plan. He lay down in the road without moving, just as if he were dead. Sure enough, before long he heard the clip-clip of a horse's hoofs, and along came a peasant driving his cart to market. And the cart was filled with butter churns.

"Hello! I see a dead wolf in the road," said the peasant. "I'll take him to market and sell his skin."

This was splendid! Everything was happening just as the Fox had said it would.

But then the peasant scratched his head and said: "How can I be sure the wolf is really dead? I don't want to get bitten when I go to pick him up! I know – I'll drive the cart over him, just to make sure."

And before the Wolf had time to get to his feet and run away, the peasant whipped up his horse and drove the cart right over his body. How the Wolf howled! How black and blue he was! He limped off into the forest, a sorrier sight than ever.

"I'll let that Fox know what I think of him!" he vowed. "Just let me meet him again – he'll find he has tricked me once too often!"

Now it was winter. The trees of the forest were bare, and snow covered the ground. The Wolf met the Fox a third time – and on this occasion the Fox was enjoying a fish. A heap of fishbones lay on the ground before him.

"Just tell me where you got all those fishes, or it will be the worse for you!" the Wolf snarled, showing his sharp fangs.

"There's no need for you to snarl at me like that," the Fox protested. "Of course I'll tell you. I'm sorry our little plan concerning the butter did not work out as well as we had hoped it would. However, if I show you where to catch a feast of fish, that will make up for it. Just follow me."

And he led the Wolf to a stream.

"Here we are," said the Fox. "All you have to do is to sit here with your tail dipped into the water. You may have to keep it in the water for some time, until a really big fish comes along. Then, as soon as you feel it tugging at your tail, whisk it out of the water – and there you are! You may feel a few nibbles from some of the smaller fish, but don't take any notice of them – it's best to wait for the really big catch, if you'll take my advice!"

Well, the Wolf sat patiently on the brink of the stream with his tail dipped into the water. He felt a few little tweaks, but took no notice, remembering the Fox's advice. Presently it became very cold, and the Wolf began to shiver. "This

28

is no good!" he thought. "I shan't fish any longer today – I'll try my luck again tomorrow. Perhaps the fish will be biting then!"

Then he tried to get up – but he found he couldn't. There seemed to be a great weight pulling on his tail.

"A big fish at last!" he cried.

He pulled and pulled – but nothing happened. He could not whisk that big fish out of the water. At last he twisted round to see what was the matter – and then he discovered the truth.

There was no big fish pulling at his tail at all. The water of the stream had frozen, and his tail was held fast in the ice! As for those little tweaks he had felt before –

why, that had been the ice forming around his tail!

So the Fox had played another trick on him! The Wolf was very angry indeed. He tugged and pulled with all his might: until at last his tail broke clean off, and he had to leave it behind him. Then he ran through the cold dark forest, seeking the Fox, and at last he found him.

"Now, see what has happened!" the Wolf howled. "All because of your bad advice. And *this* time, my fine friend—"

But the Fox interrupted him before he could finish.

"I am very sorry indeed to see that you have lost your tail," he said. "I must get you a new one at once. That is the least I can do to make amends."

The Wolf was so surprised that he forgot how angry he had been a moment before.

"Get me a new tail?" he repeated. "But that's impossible!"

"Not at all," said the Fox. "Come with me." He led the Wolf to a blacksmith's forge. "My friend here would like a new tail, if you please," he told the blacksmith.

"Certainly, anything to oblige," the blacksmith replied.

He put a bar of iron in his fire, left it until it was white-hot, and beat it into the shape of a tail. Then he fastened it to the Wolf, to take the place of the tail he had lost. The Wolf no sooner felt the red-hot iron than he uttered a fearful howl and leaped sky-high . . . up, up, up he went, far above the treetops, until he was only a distant speck among the clouds. He jumped so high that he took a very long time to come down again, and found he had landed in a strange country.

"Just let me find that Fox!" he muttered angrily. "Just let me find him!"

But alas! The Wolf did not know where to begin to look for the Fox. Besides, his iron tail was so heavy that he could only move along very slowly. For all I know, he is still looking for the sly Fox, dragging his tail behind him.

THE CAT AND HER PUPIL

At the beginning of time, the fierce Tiger was a clumsy creature, unskilled in hunting. He made so much noise as he passed through the jungle that all the other creatures could hear him coming, and had plenty of time to run away to safety. They jeered at the Tiger for his clumsiness. "You should learn to walk silently through the jungle, Lord Tiger, or you will never catch your prey!" they said mockingly.

The Tiger knew that unless he became a more skillful hunter, he would starve. Then he thought of his Cousin the Cat. The Cat was swift and silent. She prowled through the jungle like a shadow, and pounced on her prey without warning. Perhaps the Cat would teach him how to become a skillful hunter.

So the Tiger went to see the Cat. "Dear Cousin, will you teach me to hunt and catch my prey?" he asked her. "If you will show me all the secrets of your skill, I will serve you faithfully for three years."

The Cat was flattered that such a strong, fierce creature as the Tiger would want to become her pupil.

"Very well, Cousin Tiger, I will teach you the skill of hunting," she agreed, "and you shall become my servant for three years."

And that was how the Tiger became the Cat's apprentice. He ran errands at her bidding; he kept their cave clean, and prepared their meals. The Cat, for her part, showed the Tiger the secrets of her skill. She taught him how to prowl silently through the jungle; how to sniff the wind for the scent of other animals, and how to stand so still that no one would suspect his presence. The Cat and the Tiger went hunting together every day, and the Tiger proved himself an excellent pupil. He quickly mastered all that the Cat taught him. In fact, he was so good that the Cat grew quite jealous of her pupil.

"If I am not careful, the Tiger will soon become a better hunter than me!" she thought. "That would never do."

And so the Cat decided to keep to herself one special secret of her hunting skill.

At last the three years of the Tiger's apprenticeship were over.

"Now, Cousin, have you taught me all the secrets of your skill in return for my faithful service to you?" asked the Tiger.

"Indeed, I have, every one," replied the Cat. But she did not speak the truth.

The Tiger, however, was quite satisfied, and went away well pleased with the knowledge he had acquired. He began to hunt by himself. And now the other

30

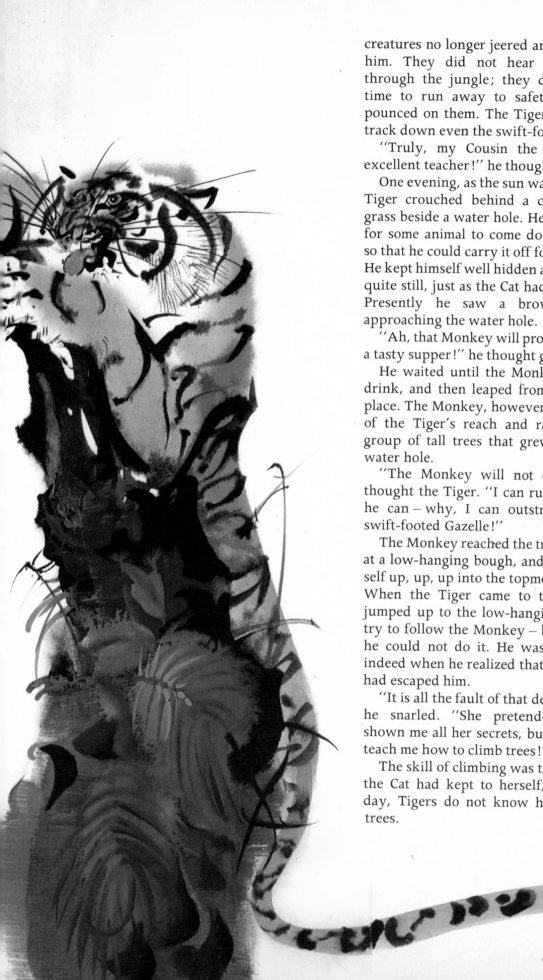

creatures no longer jeered and mocked at him. They did not hear him coming through the jungle; they did not have time to run away to safety before he pounced on them. The Tiger was able to track down even the swift-footed Gazelle.

"Truly, my Cousin the Cat was an excellent teacher!" he thought to himself.

One evening, as the sun was setting, the Tiger crouched behind a clump of tall grass beside a water hole. He was waiting for some animal to come down to drink, so that he could carry it off for his supper. He kept himself well hidden and remained quite still, just as the Cat had taught him. Presently he saw a brown Monkey approaching the water hole.

"Ah, that Monkey will provide me with a tasty supper!" he thought gleefully.

He waited until the Monkey began to drink, and then leaped from his hiding-place. The Monkey, however, twisted out of the Tiger's reach and ran toward a group of tall trees that grew beside the water hole.

"The Monkey will not escape me!" thought the Tiger. "I can run faster than he can – why, I can outstrip even the swift-footed Gazelle!"

The Monkey reached the trees, grabbed at a low-hanging bough, and swung himself up, up, up into the topmost branches. When the Tiger came to the trees, he jumped up to the low-hanging bough to try to follow the Monkey – but he found he could not do it. He was very angry indeed when he realized that the Monkey had escaped him.

"It is all the fault of that deceitful Cat!" he snarled. "She pretended she had shown me all her secrets, but she did not teach me how to climb trees!"

The skill of climbing was the one secret the Cat had kept to herself, and to this day, Tigers do not know how to climb trees.

THE WOLF WEARS A SHEEPSKIN

A hungry gray Wolf prowled around a green meadow where a flock of fine fat sheep nibbled the grass. Nearby sat their shepherd, playing his pipe and watching that no harm came to them.

"If only I could outwit the shepherd and get within the flock, I would have a fine time!" thought the Wolf.

Then he saw a curly white sheepskin lying on the ground. That gave him an idea. He put the sheepskin over his own back and crept into the midst of the flock, pretending to nibble the pasture as they were doing. The real sheep showed no alarm, and the shepherd did not notice that one of his white lambs was really a gray Wolf.

The Wolf congratulated himself. "How clever I was to think of this plan! Now, when the sun goes down and that foolish shepherd shuts the flock in the fold for the night, I will be able to enjoy a splendid feast!"

Soon the sun left the sky and dusk fell

upon the meadow. The shepherd gathered his flock together and urged them toward the fold. All the sheep went into the fold – and the Sheep-who-was-a-Wolf went with them.

The shepherd made sure the fold was secure, and blocked the entrance with a boulder.

"My plan could not have succeeded better!" thought the Wolf. "The shepherd – silly fellow – will go away in a moment, and then I will begin my feast. How hungry I am!" He ran his red tongue over his pointed yellow teeth. "Let me see – I shall start with that tender little lamb over there."

Oh yes, the Wolf was clever – but he was just too clever for his own good. As the shepherd turned away from the fold, he suddenly thought he would like some roast lamb for his supper. So he took his sharp-bladed knife, reached inside the entrance of the fold, and killed the first animal he caught. It happened to be the Wolf.

THE TIGER,
THE ELEPHANT AND
THE MONKEY

Deep in the heart of the green forest, the Elephant and the Tiger came face to face in a narrow pathway.

"Get out of my way, Elephant," said the Tiger. "I am the Lord of the Forest."

The Elephant was angry. "I acknowledge only the Lion as Lord of the Forest," he retorted. "And now I will trample you underfoot for insulting me."

"Let us hold a trial to see which of us is the mightier," suggested the Tiger. "The winner shall eat up the loser."

The Elephant agreed to this. Then the Tiger opened his mouth and gave a mighty roar that resounded through the forest. It was so loud that a Jackal who was prowling nearby died of fright when he heard it.

"I can do better than that," boasted the Elephant.

He lifted his long trunk and trumpeted for all he was worth. The trees shook at the noise, but no creature died of fright.

"Ah, Elephant," said the Tiger triumphantly, "I am the winner of the contest, and now I am going to eat you up!"

The Elephant could only agree that the Tiger had shown himself to be the mightier animal, and had therefore the right to eat him up, but he begged the Tiger to spare his life for a few days, so that he could say good-by to his wife and family.

"Very well," said the Tiger, "but be sure to return here to me in seven days time."

"I shall not forget," replied the Elephant.

Sadly he went home to his wife and their two little calves, and told them about the unhappy fate that had befallen him. Tenderly he bade his family farewell, and showed them how to find their food when he would no longer be there to look after them. And on the sixth day following his unlucky enounter with the Tiger, he set off through the forest to keep the bargain he had made. On his way he met the Rabbit.

"What is the matter with you, Elephant?" asked the Rabbit. "You look so sad and miserable."

"Alas, little Rabbit," answered the Elephant, "I have made a bargain with the Tiger, who is going to eat me up." And he told the Rabbit all about the contest they had held, and how the Jackal had died of fright when he heard the roar of the Tiger.

The Rabbit listened carefully. Then he said: "If you follow my advice, you need not lose your life, Elephant."

Then the Rabbit called a meeting of all the creatures who lived in the forest – except for the troublesome Monkey (who was always playing tricks on the other animals) and, of course, the Tiger. He asked the assembly to help him to save the Elephant's life.

"Willingly, friend Rabbit, if you will tell us what to do," said the Bear. And there were murmurs of assent from all around – from the swift-footed Deer, the Hippopotamus, the prickly Porcupine, the yellow Toad, and every other creature.

"This is what we must do," the Rabbit told them. "Tomorrow you must run through the forest in great terror, shout-

34

ing: 'The mighty Rabbit has conquered
the Elephant, and now he is searching for
the Tiger!'''

The animals agreed to do this, for they
knew the wisdom of the Rabbit, and
guessed he had thought of a good plan to
save the Elephant's life.

The next morning was the seventh day
since the Elephant had met the Tiger. At
sunrise, the Rabbit jumped on to the Elephant's back, holding a bunch of bananas.

"Now, Elephant," he said, "take me to
the place where you are to meet the Tiger."

As they went slowly into the heart of
the green forest, terror-stricken cries
arose on every side: "The mighty Rabbit
has conquered the Elephant, and now he is
searching for the Tiger!"

The Tiger was waiting for the Elephant
at their appointed meeting place. He
heard the terrified cries of the forest
animals, and was uneasy.

"How could the little Rabbit possibly
harm such mighty creatures as the Elephant and myself?" he scoffed. "Yet why
are the other animals so afraid? I hear the
cry of the Bear, the swift-footed Deer, the
Hippopotamus, the prickly Porcupine,
and the yellow Toad . . . It would be as well
to have an ally to stand beside me and
fight the Rabbit, if he has really con-

quered the Elephant and is now searching for me."

It so happened that the Monkey was sitting on the branch of a tree, above the Tiger's head. "I will help you fight the Rabbit, Tiger," he said. And he waited by the Tiger's side.

Still the cries of terror echoed throughout the forest. The Tiger and the Monkey became very worried.

"The Tiger is a treacherous animal," thought the Monkey. "For all I know, he may run away from the Rabbit and abandon me to my fate."

"The Monkey is not to be trusted," thought the Tiger. "He may take to his heels as soon as the Rabbit arrives, and leave me to fight it out alone."

"Friend Tiger," said the Monkey, "let us tie our tails together in a knot, so that we shall not be separated when the enemy appears."

"Friend Monkey," said the Tiger, "that is an excellent idea."

So they tied their two tails together.

Now they heard the plodding steps of the Elephant as he drew near. A moment later they saw him walking toward them, with the Rabbit sitting on his back eating the bananas one by one.

"Ho, Tiger!" called the Rabbit, "I am eating the brains of the Elephant, and soon I shall eat your brains as well!"

The Tiger was so ignorant that he believed the bananas really were the brains of the Elephant.

"Oh, friend Monkey, let us run away!" he cried in fear.

"How stupid you are, Tiger!" retorted the Monkey. "Those are bananas, not brains. I eat them every day, so I should know!"

Just then the Rabbit looked at the Monkey and said to him: "What is the meaning of this, Monkey? You boasted that you would bring me a big, fat Tiger to eat. This is only a small, thin Tiger."

At these words, the Tiger turned and

36

fled. "You wicked creature!" he shouted at the Monkey. "Now I see why you offered to help me fight the Rabbit, why you suggested we should tie our tails together, and why you said the brains were bananas. You pretended to be my ally, but all the time you were really helping the Rabbit!"

The Monkey had no breath to answer the Tiger's accusations, he was being pulled along at such a rate. "Stop, stop!" he cried. "I cannot run so fast as you, friend Tiger!" But the Tiger was too frightened to stop.

At last they each ran either side of a tall tree that stood in their path, and their tails were pulled so hard against the trunk that the knot was broken. Then the Tiger ran off to the hills, and the Monkey found refuge in the treetops. As for the Elephant, he went back to his wife and two little calves, thanks to the clever plan of the wise Rabbit.

THE MOUSE,
THE BIRD AND THE
SAUSAGE

You shall hear how a Mouse, a Bird and a Sausage set up house together, and what became of them. The house stood in a forest clearing, a little white house with a thatched roof. All round stood the tall trees, and in the depths of the dark forest lurked wolves and bears.

This is how the three companions looked after each other. The Bird would fly into the forest each morning to fetch wood for the fire. The Mouse would light the fire, bring water from the well, and lay the table. The Sausage did all the cooking. At first all went well, and in this way they lived together happily and contentedly. But one day when the Bird flew into the forest to gather firewood, he stopped to talk with a Crow. The Bird boasted to the Crow of his good fortune, and told him all about the excellent arrangement he had made with his friends the Mouse and the Sausage.

"Caw!" croaked the Crow. "I don't call

that a good arrangement at all. If you ask me, you have by far the worst of the bargain. Here you are, hard at work gathering firewood, while the Mouse and the Sausage stay comfortably at home. I daresay the Mouse retires for a nap as soon as she has lit the fire and drawn the water and laid the table. As for the Sausage – what a lazy fellow he must be! All he does is to watch the cooking pot, and when it is time for dinner, he just rolls himself through the vegetables once or twice, and there they are – buttered, salted, and ready to eat. I don't call that hard work, do you?''

The Bird listened to the Crow's advice. He began to think that what he said must be true. And the next day, when it was time for him to fly into the forest to fetch the firewood, he said to the Mouse and the Sausage:

''I've done enough of the hard work in this house! I know what an easy time you two have while I fly off into the forest. We must come to another arrangement. I refuse to gather firewood any more.''

The Mouse and the Sausage looked at him in dismay. Everything had gone along so smoothly until this moment. They each did their own share of the work about the house, and no one had complained till now. However, they agreed to cast lots. The Bird collected three twigs. Whoever drew the longest twig would gather firewood; he who drew the middle twig would light the fire, draw water, and lay the table. And the one who drew the shortest twig would do the cooking.

This is the way it came out: The Sausage was to gather firewood. The Bird was to light the fire, draw water, and lay the table. The Mouse was to do the cooking.

The Sausage set off into the forest. Alas! He had not gone very far before he met a hungry Wolf, who gobbled him up before he had time to bid him ''good day.'' So that was the end of the Sausage.

The Bird, meanwhile, lit the fire and then went to draw water from the well. ''The Mouse did not have such an easy

time of it after all!'' he thought as he hauled on the chain to bring up the heavy bucket. Alas! Just as the bucket came level with the top of the well, it slipped from the Bird's claws, and in trying to recover it he fell right down into the water and was drowned. So that was the end of the Bird.

What of the Mouse? Unaware of what had befallen her two friends, she watched the cooking pot and stirred the vegetables. When it was time for dinner, she remembered that the Sausage used to roll among the vegetables in the pot in order to butter and salt them ready for eating. So she decided to do the same. Alas! No sooner had she crept into the cooking pot than she was boiled and scalded. So that was the end of the Mouse.

And now the little house in the forest clearing stood empty, for there was no one left to live in it. And yet, if only the Bird had not listened to bad advice, the three companions might be living there still.

THE CUNNING
JACKAL

For many weeks the hot sun had shone down on the land. The ground was parched, and the streams had all dried up. Many of the jungle animals died of thirst before the rains fell once more. The Lion called all his subjects together, and told them that they must think of a plan to prevent such a terrible drought happening again. For a long time the animals sat in silence. Then the hairy Ape spoke.

"Let us all go to live in a country where rain falls all the year round," he suggested.

Some of the other creatures thought this was a sensible idea, but the wrinkled Tortoise objected to it.

"Such a country would be so far away that I could never live long enough to complete the journey," he said.

"Why should we not sleep all through the next dry season?" hissed the slithery Snake.

"That wouldn't suit me at all!" cried the frisky Hare. "I would die of starvation."

So the discussion continued, until at last two of the most cunning creatures of all, the Hyena and the Jackal, suggested that they should all join in digging a deep hole, to hold enough water to last through the next dry season.

So the very next day, all the animals came to dig the hole. It was agreed that they would each take their turn, and that as the Hyena and the Jackal had thought of the plan, the Hyena should dig first, and the Jackal last. They set to work, and each creature dug in turn – the Hyena, the Ape, the Elephant, the Monkey, King Lion himself, and all the other animals that lived in the jungle. By now the hole was deep and wide. And now it was the Jackal's turn to dig. But the Jackal was nowhere to be found! At last the Lion decreed they must finish the digging without him.

"Let the Elephant dig a second time," he said. "That is only fair, since he drinks

40

twice as much water as the rest of us!''

So the hole was finished, and soon the rain began to fall, and filled it to the brim with pure, sweet water.

"No one may drink here except those who have helped to dig the hole," said the Lion.

The cunning Jackal, who had been too lazy to take his turn at digging, was hiding in the bushes. He heard the Lion's words, and very early next morning, before any other creature was about, he crept down to the hole and drank his fill.

"So much for you, King Lion!" he laughed.

This went on for some time; every morning the Jackal came down to drink, and no one discovered him. One hot morning, he grew bolder still, and swam in the hole, stirring up the water and making it muddy. When the other animals saw it, they were angry.

"Who did this?" demanded the Lion.

But no one knew.

The Tortoise was very wise. "I know what we must do," he said. "Cover my shell with a coating of beeswax to make it sticky. Then I will watch all night and catch the culprit."

So they covered the Tortoise's shell with a thick coat of sticky beeswax, and he lurked by the hole to watch for the trespasser. He drew his wrinkled head and his wrinkled feet and his little pointed tail inside his shell, so that he looked just like a brown stone. Every now and then he poked his head out slowly to see if anyone was coming. The long night passed. And just as dawn came, the Tortoise heard a noise in the bushes. He stayed very still

41

and waited to see what would happen.

The Jackal came sauntering out of the bushes.

"I think I will take another dip in the water hole today after I have drunk my fill," he said to himself.

By the side of the water hole he saw a brown stone.

"What a convenient steppingstone!" he thought. And he put his two forefeet on the Tortoise's shell, and bent down to have a drink before he plunged in. Imagine his surprise when he found his feet stuck fast in the sticky beeswax!

"Let me go! Let me go! This is a mean trick!" he howled.

"One mean trick deserves another," the Tortoise told him; and he began to move slowly away from the water hole.

"If you don't let me go, I will kick your shell to pieces with my two hind feet!" yelled the Jackal.

"Go ahead," said the Tortoise, still walking along.

So the Jackal kicked the Tortoise as hard as he could with his two hind feet. But all that happened was that they, too, stuck fast in the sticky beeswax!

"If you don't let me go at once, I will bite you in two!" threatened the Jackal menacingly.

"Just try it," said the Tortoise.

The Jackal opened his mouth to bite the Tortoise's shell in two – and this time his jaws stuck fast in the sticky beeswax! Now he could no longer call out and make threats, and the Tortoise carried him slowly along into the heart of the jungle.

All the other animals gathered there to see the cunning Jackal stuck fast to the Tortoise's shell, and the Lion praised the Tortoise for his wisdom. Then he decreed that the Jackal must die for his laziness and dishonesty. He told the Hyena to seize the Jackal by his tail, swing him round, and dash him against a tree trunk. Then he said to the Jackal:

"Before you die, however, you may enjoy one last meal. For that is a favor granted to every criminal condemned to death."

When the Jackal heard the Lion's words, his cunning mind at once began to contrive how he might escape this dreadful fate that lay in store for him. He ate the good meal which was put before him, and when no one was looking, he took a lump of fat and greased his tail all the way to the tip, so that it was as slippery as a piece of wet soap. A sly grin then spread over his face.

"Now, Jackal, are you ready?" asked the Lion.

"I am ready," replied the Jackal. "But may I make a suggestion? I think the other animals who have come to see me die should sit as far away as possible. Otherwise when the Hyena lets go of me, I might hit one of them instead of the tree, and I wouldn't want a nasty accident like that to happen."

The Lion thought this was a sensible idea, and so all the animals went as far away as they could without being out of sight of the execution.

Then the Hyena seized the Jackal by his tail and began to swing him round his head with all his might. But what happened? The harder he swung him, the more quickly the Jackal's greasy tail slithered out of his hand! Try as he might, the Hyena just couldn't keep hold of the slippery tail, and in another second the Jackal had slipped from his grasp, and was running away through the jungle as fast as he could. The Hyena fell to the ground with a bump, and the other animals were all so far away that by the time they began to chase the Jackal, it was far too late to catch up with him.

So the Jackal escaped – but he never came down to the water hole again. And to this day, you will find a wise Tortoise beside every water hole in the jungle, on guard against any trespasser who might be tempted to steal the water.

THE QUARREL

On a hot, dusty day a Lion and a Boar came to the same water hole. In the soft ground all round the water hole there were the tracks of many creatures: deer and goats, foxes and jackals, elephant and rhino. None of these other creatures would have come to the water hole at the same time as the Lion; they were too much afraid of him. But the fierce Boar, with his sharp tusks, was as strong as the Lion with his cruel claws.

The Boar plunged down to the water's edge, but before he could put down his head to drink, the Lion came and pushed him aside in his eagerness to get to the water.

"I was here before you – I will drink first!" snorted the Boar furiously.

"Get out of my way! You can drink after I have had my fill!" the Lion snarled.

"If you don't wait your turn, I will tear you to pieces with my sharp tusks," the Boar threatened.

"Unless you get out of my way, I will claw you to ribbons," retorted the Lion.

Forthwith they fell to battle, each determined to fight to the death. The Boar rushed at the Lion and gored his flanks until the blood flowed freely. The Lion sprang upon the Boar and mauled him until he could scarcely stand his ground.

Suddenly there was a rustling among the treetops. Looking up, the Lion and the Boar spied a number of black vultures settling in the branches above them, waiting to devour whichever of them was killed. This sinister sight soon put an end to their quarrel.

"Let us call a truce," said the Lion. "It is better for us to be friends than to provide a feast for those birds of prey."

The Boar heartily agreed with the Lion – and so, licking their wounds, they took it in turns to drink their fill, and parted friends.

44

TIT FOR TAT

A Camel and a Jackal once struck up a friendship. But, as is the way of all good things, their friendship came to an end one day, and this is how it happened.

The Jackal said to the Camel: "I have heard that there is a big field of sugar cane on the other side of the wide river. Would you like me to show you where it is?"

Now there was nothing the Camel liked to eat more than sweet, sticky sugar cane. "Yes, please show me where it is, my friend!" he begged the Jackal.

"The only thing is that we will have to cross the river to get there," said the Jackal. "That presents no problem for you, for you are able to swim. But I cannot swim."

"Then I will take you on my back," offered the Camel.

"Excellent," agreed the Jackal.

And so the Camel swam across the wide river with the Jackal sitting on his humpy back. When they reached the other side, the Jackal showed the Camel where the field of sugar cane lay, and the Camel set off eagerly.

"I will stay here on the shore until you come back," the Jackal told him. "There are plenty of crabs and fishbones to provide a meal for me. I enjoy that sort of thing."

Now the Jackal was an impatient creature. He soon ate his fill of crabs and fishbones, and grew tired of waiting for the Camel to return. So he went up to the field of sugar cane to find out why his friend was being so long. He had forgotten that the Camel, who was a much larger animal than himself, needed more food to satisfy his appetite. Moreover, unlike the Jackal, who gulped his food down, the Camel chewed over every mouthful. So, although the Jackal had quickly finished his meal on the shore, the Camel was only just beginning his feast in the sugar cane field.

46

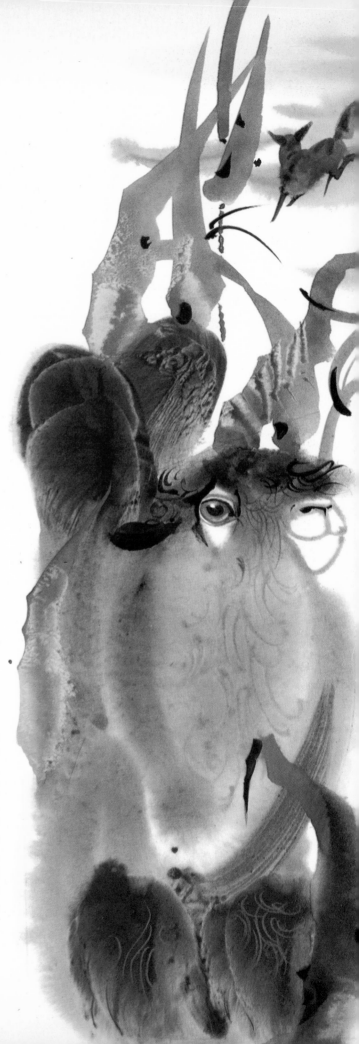

"Hurry up, old friend! Make haste, slowpoke!" yelped the Jackal.

The Camel did not like to be hurried. "I will come in my own good time," he replied haughtily, and went on eating.

This made the Jackal very annoyed indeed. He began to bark angrily, and then ran round and round the sugar cane field, howling as loudly as he could.

A little distance away was a village. When the villagers heard the noise the Jackal was making, they said: "There is a Jackal among the sugar canes; he will scratch holes in the ground, and spoil the roots of the plants."

Then they all gathered together in a band, and came banging pots and kettles, to drive the Jackal away. But when they got there, they found, not only a Jackal, but a Camel as well, busily eating the succulent sugar canes! They were so annoyed that they ignored the Jackal and set about beating the Camel with sticks. The poor Camel was driven from the field, bruised all over.

At last the villagers went away. Then the Camel turned to the Jackal and said: "Why did you run round the field making all that noise, my friend? Look what happened! You roused the villagers, and they have beaten me black and blue!"

The Jackal didn't seem at all sorry for what he had done. "I couldn't help it," he said sulkily. "It's just a custom I have. I always like to sing and dance after I've eaten."

The Camel gave him a queer look. Then he said: "We had better be getting home. Jump on my back and we will return across the river."

The Jackal jumped on the Camel's humpy back, just as he had done before, and the Camel began to swim across the wide river. He had just reached the very deepest part when he said: "I really feel I would like to roll in the water, my friend."

The Jackal was most alarmed to hear this. "Don't do that, whatever you do!" he begged the Camel. "I would fall off your back and be drowned! You know I can't swim!"

"I really would like to roll in the water very much," repeated the Camel.

"Why are you so anxious to roll in the water?" asked the Jackal.

Then the Camel said airily: "Oh, it's just a custom I have. I always like to roll in the water after I've eaten."

And with that he rolled over in the water, so that the Jackal fell off his back and was drowned. And that was the end of their friendship.

HOW THE CAT AND
THE MOUSE
BECAME ENEMIES

A long, long time ago, when the world was young and animals were able to talk to each other as human beings do today, a mother Cat once took her kitten into the middle of a corn field, where they lay and basked in the hot sun. In those far-off days the sun always seemed to shine much brighter than it does today, and very soon the little kitten was fast asleep. Before long, a timid Deer came by on her way to the forest. Suddenly she heard a loud noise. It was only the sound of a Woodpecker tapping on a tree trunk, but the Deer was so frightened that she leaped in the air. She landed right on top of the little kitten, and it began to cry.

"How dare you step on my kitten!" the mother Cat said crossly.

"I'm very sorry," answered the Deer. "I didn't mean to hurt your kitten. You see, I got such a fright when I heard the noise the Woodpecker made that I jumped in the air. You know what a timid creature I am."

"Humph," said the mother Cat, "so it was the Woodpecker's fault."

She decided to find the Woodpecker and tell him what she thought of him. She soon saw him clinging to a tree trunk.

"I know it was all because of you that the Deer stepped on my kitten and made it cry!" she called up to him angrily. "The noise you made with your pecking frightened her so much that she jumped in the air."

The Woodpecker looked down at the Cat in astonishment. "How could I know that the noise of my pecking would frighten the Deer? In any case, I only pecked the tree because the Colibri bird came to visit me and show me his forked tail. He asked me to peck the tree."

"Humph!" said the mother Cat, "so it was the fault of the Colibri bird!"

And off she went to find him. Pretty soon she found him sitting on a bush.

"You nasty Colibri bird!" she exclaimed. "If you hadn't gone to visit the Woodpecker and show him your forked tail, he would not have pecked the tree and frightened the Deer so that she jumped in the air and landed on top of my kitten."

The little Colibri bird felt insulted.

"It has nothing to do with me," he said huffily. "If you want to pin the blame on someone, you should go to see the Rice Bird. I only went to visit my cousin the Woodpecker because when I called on the Rice Bird he was crying, and did not want to look at my forked tail."

"Humph," said the mother Cat, "so it was really the fault of the Rice Bird!"

She walked through the forest to the river bank, and found the Rice Bird on a bough.

"It's you who are the cause of all the mischief!" the Cat scolded him. "If you had not been crying when the Colibri Bird came to show you his forked tail, he would not have gone to visit the Woodpecker, and the Woodpecker would not have pecked the tree and frightened the Deer, so that she stepped on my poor little kitten and made it cry!"

The Rice Bird listened to the Cat's scolding and then replied: "Don't blame me, friend Cat. It is true I was crying when the Colibri bird came to see me, but that was because the Crab came scuttling up and tried to cut off the yellow stripe around my neck with her sharp pincers."

"Humph," said the Cat. "So the Crab is the real culprit!"

She soon found the Crab, who was lurking behind a large stone.

"It's no use hiding behind that stone," the Cat told her. "I know it was all because of you that my poor little kitten was hurt. If you had not tried to cut off the Rice Bird's yellow stripe with your sharp pincers, he would not have cried, the Colibri bird would not have visited the Woodpecker, and the Woodpecker would not have pecked the tree and frightened the Deer so that she leaped in the air and landed on my kitten."

When the Crab heard this long speech of the Cat's, she was indignant. "How dare you come here and accuse me of such a thing!" she cried. "In any case, I only scuttled up to the Rice Bird because I was being chased by the brown Mouse — so *he* is the one you should talk to!"

"Humph," said the mother Cat. "So the brown Mouse is at the bottom of it all, is he?"

And off she set to find the Mouse. He was not by the river bank. He was not in the forest. Where do you think she found him? Why, in the very field where she had been basking in the sun with her kitten! He was nibbling an ear of corn.

"At last I have come to the end of my search!" the mother Cat said to him. "*You* are the wretch whose fault it all is! You chased the Crab, who tried to cut off the Rice Bird's yellow stripe with her sharp pincers and made him cry, so that the Colibri bird went to see the Woodpecker, who pecked the tree and frightened the Deer so that she leaped in the air and landed on my kitten and made her cry!"

The poor little brown Mouse was so surprised when he heard this rigmarole that he could not utter one single squeak. His silence convinced the Cat that he was indeed the guilty one – so she sprang upon him and ate him.

And from that day forward the Cat and the Mouse became bitter enemies.

HENNY-PENNY

One summer's day, a long, long time ago, a little red Hen was picking up peas in her beak in the farmyard, when all of a sudden a pea fell *plonk* right on top of her head.

"Goodness gracious!" cried the little red Hen, "the sky is falling down!"

She got in a dreadful commotion, flapping her wings and squawking for all she was worth. And she thought she must go to the King's castle, to tell the King that the sky was falling down. So off she trotted through the farmyard, and on her way she met the Cock, with his fine scarlet comb and handsome tailfeathers.

"Where are you going in such a hurry, Henny-Penny?" asked the Cock.

"Oh, Cocky-Locky, the sky is falling down, and I am going to the King's castle to tell the King!"

"I will come with you, Henny-Penny!" said the Cock; and off he strutted by her side.

A little farther on they met a plump white Duck with an orange beak.

"Where are you going in such a hurry, Cocky-Locky and Henny-Penny?" asked the Duck.

"Oh, Ducky-Daddles, the sky is falling down, and we are going to the King's castle to tell the King!"

"I will go with you, Cocky-Locky and Henny-Penny!" said the Duck; and off she waddled alongside them.

Whom should they meet next but the big gray Goose.

"Where are you going in such a hurry, Ducky-Daddles, Cocky-Locky and Henny-Penny?" asked the Goose.

"Oh, Goosey-Poosey, the sky is falling down, and we are going to tell the King!"

"I will go with you, Ducky-Daddles, Cocky-Locky, and Henny-Penny!" said the Goose; and off she strode behind them.

50

Now they came to a green field where the red-wattled Turkey was busy gobbling the tender grass.

"Where are you going in such a hurry, Goosey-Poosey, Ducky-Daddles, Cocky-Locky and Henny-Penny?" asked the Turkey.

"Oh, Turkey-Lurkey, the sky is falling down, and we are going to the King's castle to tell the King!"

"I will go with you, Goosey-Poosey, Ducky-Daddles, Cocky-Locky, and Henny-Penny!" said the Turkey; and off he marched at the end of the procession.

So Turkey-Lurkey, Goosey-Poosey, Ducky-Daddles, Cocky-Locky and Henny-Penny went on together. They left the farmyard behind them, and straggled across the hill where the red-brown fox lived. The Fox saw them coming, and he licked his lips as he went to meet them.

"Good-day, Turkey-Lurkey, Goosey-Poosey, Ducky-Daddles, Cocky-Locky, and Henny-Penny!" he greeted them most politely. "And where might you be going?"

"Good-day, Mr. Fox! The sky is falling down, and we are going to the King's castle to tell the King!"

Then the Fox said: "Do you know the way to the King's castle? Come with me, and I will show you."

So the five foolish feathered fowls followed the red-brown Fox over the hill to the den where he lived with his wife and their little cubs.

"This is the King's castle!" said the crafty Fox.

And the five foolish feathered fowls went into the Fox's hole, one after another, and the Fox's wife and their little cubs ate up first poor Henny-Penny, then poor Cocky-Locky, then poor Ducky-Daddles, then Goosey-Poosey, and then Turkey-Lurkey; and so they never reached the King to tell him that the sky was falling down!

51

THE FOX AND THE CROW

A Carrion Crow was perched in a tree. In his beak he held a piece of meat. He had flown into the tree to enjoy it in peace.

Presently, however, a Fox came by. He looked up and saw the Crow with his juicy tidbit. His mouth watered. He was determined to get that piece of meat for himself, by pitting his wits against the Crow's.

"Good day to you, Sir Crow!" called the Fox. "What a beautiful big bird you are, to be sure! What a lovely blue-black sheen your glossy feathers have! How often I have admired you as you fly through the air beating your strong wings."

Now the Carrion Crow is an astute bird. He looked down at the Fox suspiciously, and wondered why he was flattering him. "Ha! Friend Fox must be after this piece of meat I hold in my beak," he thought to himself. "But he needn't try his crafty ways with me. I'm up to all his tricks!"

The Fox walked round the tree, waving his bushy red tail.

"Truly, Sir Crow, you should be king of all the birds. What are the others compared with you? The Eagle does not fly more swiftly, the Hawk is not a better hunter, the Swan is not more graceful than you!"

In spite of himself, the Crow was pleased by the Fox's speech. He preened himself and his beady eyes grew bright. Perhaps what the Fox said was true! The Crow forgot that he was a slow, ungainly creature that fed upon carrion. Perhaps he should indeed be the king of all the birds!

But still he kept tight hold of the meat.

The Fox was becoming impatient. He put his head on one side as he looked up.

"You have only one fault, Sir Crow, and that is your voice. If only you had a voice to compare with the Nightingale, or the Lark, I expect you would have been chosen as king of all the birds long ago."

At this the Crow ruffled his feathers angrily.

How dared the Fox criticize his voice! What was wrong with it? The Fox did not know what he was talking about. He could sing just as well as the Nightingale or the Lark!

And then, just to prove that his voice was as good as theirs, the Crow opened his beak. "Caw! Caw!" he croaked.

Alas! The piece of meat dropped out of his beak and fell to the ground. The waiting Fox pounced on it and snapped it up.

"Caw! Caw!" croaked the Carrion Crow. "You rascal! You flatterer!"

"Don't despair, Sir Crow," said the Fox, swallowing the last morsel of that delicious tidbit, "for who knows – if you add wisdom to all your other qualifications, you may yet make an ideal king!"

And he ran off, licking his lips and grinning at his own cleverness in outwitting the Crow.

THE WOLF AND THE SEVEN LITTLE KIDS

Once upon a time there was a Nanny Goat who had seven little kids. They lived in a tiny white house on the edge of the forest. The Nanny Goat loved her little kids very dearly, and looked after them with tender care. They were all very happy in their little home, but Nanny Goat did sometimes wish that the seven little kids had a father to look after them. It wasn't because they were naughty – at least, they were no naughtier than other little kids – but because she feared for their safety. One day she had to go into the forest to get food for them.

Before she set out, she called all seven kids to her and said:

"Now, children, I must leave you for a while. When I am gone, be on your guard against the bad gray Wolf. If you let him into the house, he will eat you all up, every morsel! The Wolf is clever, and often disguises himself. But you will know him by his deep rough voice and black feet. So beware, dear children!"

The little kids replied: "Don't worry, Mother dear, we will take good care."

So their mother left the house and went off into the forest. She had not been gone long when there was a loud knock and the seven little kids heard a voice call out:

"Open the door, dear children! Your mother is here and has brought something nice for each one of you."

But the voice was deep and rough, and the little kids knew it was really the Wolf at the door. "You are not our mother!" they cried. "She has a soft, pleasant voice. You are the Wolf!"

So the Wolf slunk away with an empty belly. But he was full of cunning. He went to a shop and bought a big lump of chalk, which he ate to make his voice soft and pleasant. Then he came back to the house and knocked on the door a second time.

"Open the door, dear children! Your mother is here and has brought something nice for each one of you."

"Surely that is our mother's voice," bleated the seven little kids; and they ran to the door.

But the Wolf had laid his black paws on the window sill, and the little kids caught sight of them.

"You are not our mother!" they cried. "Her feet are not black. You are the Wolf!"

So once more the Wolf slunk away with an empty belly. But he was more cunning yet; he went to a baker's shop, and said: "I have hurt my feet. Rub some dough over them to make a poultice."

The baker did this, and then the Wolf ran to the miller. "Cover my feet with white flour!" he said.

The miller thought to himself, "The Wolf is up to no good," but as he hesitated, the Wolf said: "If you refuse to do as I ask, I will eat you!" So then the miller was afraid, and made his paws white for him.

And now the Wolf came to the little white house on the edge of the forest a third time.

"Open the door, dear children! Your mother has come home at last, and has

brought something nice for each one of you.''

The little kids cried: ''First show us your paws, so that we may see if you are really our own mother.''

Then the Wolf laid his paws on the window sill, and the little kids saw that they were as white as snow.

''Welcome home, mother dear!'' they bleated joyfully, and opened wide the door.

Who should come in but the bad gray Wolf, grinning at the success of his wicked plan! The seven little kids were dreadfully frightened. They ran about the house bleating piteously and trying to find places to hide. One crept under the table; the second jumped into the stove: the third leaped into the bedclothes; the fourth ran into the kitchen, the fifth into a cupboard, the sixth squeezed himself into the big washing bowl, and the seventh and youngest kid in the grandfather clock. But the Wolf found them all, every one . . . except for the seventh and youngest, who lay trembling inside the clock case. He swallowed all six of his brothers and sisters, and then took himself off to enjoy a good sleep after such an enormous meal.

Soon after this the mother Goat came home from the forest. What a terrible sight met her eyes! The house door stood wide open. The table and stove lay upturned; the pillows and blankets had been pulled off the bed; the kitchen was upside down, and the big washing bowl was broken in pieces. And of her seven little kids, not one could she find. She called them all by name, one after another, but there was no answer . . . until she came to the seventh and youngest. And now she heard a muffled voice saying: ''Mother, I am inside the grandfather clock!''

She opened the clock case and let out the seventh little kid, who told her everything that had happened, how the Wolf had come and swallowed up all his brothers and sisters.

You can imagine how the mother Goat wept and wailed when she learned the fate of her children. At last she went outside, and the youngest kid ran along behind her. Sadly she walked down to a meadow where yellow buttercups and scarlet poppies grew. And there, stretched out under a leafy tree, snoring his head off, lay – the Wolf! As the mother Goat gazed upon the monster who had swallowed her six children, she saw something heaving and struggling beneath the skin of his swollen stomach.

"Dear heaven!" she bleated. "Is it possible my poor children are still alive?"

She told the youngest kid to run home and fetch a pair of scissors and a needle and thread. When he returned, she took the scissors and snipped at the Wolf's stomach. No sooner had she made an opening in the skin than one little kid sprang out, alive and well, and he was followed by all the others. The greedy Wolf had swallowed them whole!

Joyfully the little kids embraced their dear mother, whose happiness knew no bounds. And still the Wolf snored as he slept under the tree.

Then the mother Goat said: "Go and fetch six big stones, children dear."

Quickly the little kids brought six big stones, and these their mother put inside the Wolf's stomach. Then she took her needle and thread and sewed him up again. And still the Wolf snored and slept.

The mother Goat and her seven little kids went home, and at last the Wolf woke up. He felt thirsty after his long sleep, and he got up to drink from a well nearby. When he began to walk, his belly rumbled and rattled so much that he cried: "Dear me! Those little kids I ate for my dinner weigh down my stomach like six big stones!"

He came to the well, and stooped down to lap the water. But the heavy stones made him lose his balance, and he fell right into the well and was drowned. Such was the end of the bad gray Wolf. And when the seven little kids heard the *splash* as he fell into the water, they came running to the well and danced around it, singing joyfully: "The Wolf is dead! The Wolf is dead!"

THE UNLUCKY GOAT

It was a hot summer day. The sun stood high in the clear blue sky and blazed down upon the earth. A Fox came running across a cornfield, where a water tank stood in the shade of a green hedge. The Fox was thirsty, and when he saw the water tank he decided to have a drink. He climbed on the edge of the tank and put down his head to drink the clear water. But the edge of the tank was slimy and slippery. Suddenly the Fox overbalanced and fell *splash* into the water. He paddled round, thrashing about with his feet, but he could not get out. He was trapped in the tank. He knew that if the farmer who owned the cornfield were to find him, he would show no mercy. Only yesterday, the Fox had got among the farmer's sheep and killed a lamb. And last week he had carried off a plump chicken . . . No, unless he could get out of the water tank, his hours were numbered.

A few moments later, a white Billy Goat with strong horns on his head and a fine silky beard under his chin entered the cornfield. He, too, was parched with thirst, and decided to take a drink from the water tank. Imagine his surprise when he looked into the tank and saw the Fox swimming about inside it!

"Good day, friend Fox," said the Goat. "Tell me, is the water in this tank good to drink?"

The Fox grinned up at the Goat's silly face. "It is excellent water, brother Goat. In fact, it is quite the best water I have ever tasted. That is why I got right inside the tank, so that I could drink as much as I wanted at my ease. But come and join me and taste some for yourself – there is plenty for both of us."

Without stopping to think, the Goat jumped right into the tank. He lapped the water greedily, and did not raise his head until his thirst was quenched.

"You were right, friend Fox," he

56

bleated, his beard dripping. "I have never tasted such excellent water!"

The Fox smiled. "Now, brother Goat, we must consider how we are to get out of this tank."

"How indeed!" echoed the Goat, looking up at the high, smooth sides of the tank.

"I have a good plan," said the Fox. "But we will need to work together if it is to succeed."

"I will do anything to help," the Goat bleated eagerly.

"In that case," said the Fox, "be so kind as to place your forefeet against the side of the tank, and hold your horns straight up. Then I can quickly climb over you, and when I am safely out of the tank, I can pull you up, too."

Willingly the Goat did as the Fox had suggested. The Fox climbed nimbly up the Goat's haunches, shoulders, and horns, and finally levered himself over the edge of the tank on to dry land once more. He shook the water out of the red-brown coat. The sun would soon dry him.

The Goat called to him from inside the tank.

"What about me, friend Fox? Don't forget our bargain! I helped you to get out, and now you must pull me up, too!"

The Fox looked into the tank, and gazed down scornfully at the Goat.

"You, brother Goat, have more hairs in your beard than brains in your head. It is your own fault that you find yourself left in that water tank – you should have stopped to think how you were going to get out again before you jumped in. *I* have no intention of pulling you out!"

At this the Goat set up a plaintive bleating, but the Fox just sauntered away across the cornfield, and was soon out of earshot.

THE WISE ANT

It was summer time. The sun shone all day long. The corn ripened in the fields, the trees were heavy with fruit, and the flowers were filled with nectar. The insects had no trouble in finding food; it was there for the taking. The Butterfly dawdled idly in the warm air, the Cicada clung indolently to a leaf, singing his shrill song and enjoying the golden sunshine.

But the wise Ant was busy. She spent the summer days scuttling about the cornfields, collecting grains of wheat and barley to store against the coming of winter.

"It is hot and sunny now," she thought, "but presently it will be cold and wet. Snow and ice will cover the earth, and there will be no food to be had."

The Beetle was foolish. He spent the summer days sunning his glossy black body on top of a flat stone. He watched the Ant as she ran busily about gathering her food, and laughed at her scornfully.

"Why do you bother to work so hard?" he jeered. "Don't you know that this is the summer time, when all creatures rest from their labors?"

The Ant was too busy to reply to the Beetle. She did not even glance at him as she hurried by with another load of barley for her store.

Now Winter came. Cold winds lashed the land. Rain fell from the sky. Snow covered the ground. Ice crusted the water.

In vain the Beetle went out to seek for something to eat. There was not a morsel of food to be found. He was famished. At last, shivering and starving, he came to the Ant's nest. The Ant sat guarding her precious hoard of food, the grains of wheat and barley she had collected all summer long.

"Give me some of your food!" begged the Beetle. "I shall die of hunger!"

The Ant looked at him scornfully. "I have no food to spare," she replied. "You should have worked as I did during the summer, and gathered your own store of food for the winter. Instead, you lay on top of a stone doing nothing, and sneered at me for my industry. It is not my fault if you starve."

The Beetle crept sadly away, and before long what he had feared came to pass, and he died of hunger.

THE SPIDER AND THE HYENA

Furry black Spider with his long spindly legs was cunning and clever. One day he went to the cave where Hyena lived with her three little cubs. Spider knew that Hyena had gone into the jungle, leaving her cubs alone. He crept right inside the cave, and began to talk to the cubs.

"What is your name?" he asked one.

"Mohammadu," the cub replied.

"And what is your name?" Spider asked the second cub.

"Isa."

"And what do they call *you*?" he asked the third cub.

"Na-taala," answered the third little Hyena.

"Now," said Spider, "you must understand that I have come to live here beside you in this warm, dark, dry cave, and so you had better know my name too. It is For-You-All."

And then he crept into a corner and waited while the three little cubs went on playing together. Presently their mother came back to the cave with some delicious food that she had found. The three cubs rushed toward her. "Who is it for?" they yelped eagerly.

"For you all," replied their mother, as she went out once more.

When the cubs heard their mother's reply, they thought she had brought all the food for the furry black stranger who had come to share their warm, dry, dark cave – and so Spider ate the best meal he had enjoyed for days. And thus it went on: each time the mother Hyena brought food to the cave, she would call out: "For you all!" and Spider gorged himself while the poor little cubs got nothing to eat at all.

One bright day, however, the mother Hyena said to her cubs: "Come out into the sunlight, children, so that I may see you."

When the three little cubs crept out of the cave, one after the other, their mother was horrified to see how wasted they were.

"What has happened to you, children!" she exclaimed. "Why are you so thin?"

"You do not bring any food for us, Mother," the cubs replied.

"But I have brought plenty of food to the cave each day," their mother protested.

"Yes, but For-You-All has eaten it up, every scrap," the cubs told her sadly.

"For-You-All? Who is that?" asked their mother.

"Why, he is the furry black stranger who shares our cave with us," said the cubs.

"Let him come out and show himself!" howled the Hyena.

Spider was crouching in his corner. He heard the Hyena's command and knew it was time he left to find another home. So he went to the mouth of the cave and pushed forward his long ears.

"Here I am!" he called. "Catch hold of my boots and pull!"

The Hyena seized hold of Spider's ears, and thinking they were boots, she pulled, and pulled, and threw them far behind her. But of course she had really pulled out Spider himself, and she had thrown him such a distance that he was able to make his escape.

"There he goes! That was For-You-All!" cried the three little cubs.

Immediately the mother Hyena gave chase, but though she searched all day, she did not find the Spider.

THE DOG AND THE SPARROW

A sorry-looking Sheepdog came shambling along the dusty high road. His head drooped, he was so thin that his ribs stuck out, and his tail hung low. A little brown Sparrow perching in the hedgerow called out:

"What is the matter, friend? Why do you look so sorry for yourself?"

"Alas," answered the Dog, "my master the shepherd is so cruel that I have run away from him. I have had nothing to eat all day, and I am very hungry."

The Sparrow felt sorry for the Dog. She flew down on to the road. "Come with me into the town, and I will find you something to eat," she said.

So the Dog and the Sparrow together followed the road until they reached the town, with its cobbled streets and red-roofed houses. There were not many people about, for it was the dinner hour, and they were all taking their afternoon naps. Presently the two friends passed by a butcher's shop, where juicy cuts of meat were displayed. The butcher, like all the other townfolk, was enjoying forty winks. His sharp knife lay idle on the chopping board, and his blue-and-white striped apron hung on a peg.

"Just wait here," the Sparrow told the Dog, "and I will get you a piece of meat."

The Dog waited, his mouth watering. The Sparrow alighted on a succulent joint and pecked and scratched at it with her beak and claws until a fine steak fell down. The Dog snatched it up in his jaws and devoured it eagerly.

"That was good!" he said, licking his lips.

"Have you had enough now?" asked the Sparrow.

"I have had plenty of meat," replied the Dog, "but I should like to eat a piece of bread after it."

"There is a baker's shop next door," said the Sparrow, "so that should not be difficult."

In the baker's shop there were trays filled with crusty loaves, currant buns and bread rolls. The Sparrow pecked at two rolls that lay on the edge of one of the trays until they fell down. The Dog gobbled them up.

"Have you eaten your fill now?" asked the Sparrow.

"Yes," said the Dog, "my stomach is full and my hunger has gone. Now let us take a walk outside the town, my friend."

They walked back to the dusty high road. The weather was warm, and soon the Dog began to yawn. "I think I will take a little nap," he said sleepily.

"Very well," answered the Sparrow. "I will perch on this bush."

The Dog stretched himself out on the road, and soon fell fast asleep. Suddenly there came the clip-clop of a horse's hoofs and the rumbling of wheels, and a cart laden with casks of wine rounded a bend in the road. The Sparrow realized that her friend the Dog lay right in the path of the cart, which came straight on toward him.

"Stop, stop, Mr. Carter!" she twittered. "Stop, I say, or things will turn out the worse for you!"

But the Carter took no notice. "How could you, a little brown bird of no importance, make it the worse for me?" he called contemptuously. He drove straight on, and the heavy wheels of the cart crushed the poor Dog to death.

"Oh!" cried the Sparrow, "you are a wicked man. You have killed my friend the Dog. Now heed my words: you shall pay for this cruel deed with all you possess."

The Carter only laughed. He cracked his whip and drove on. But the Sparrow flew after him, crept on to the cart, and pecked at one of the casks of wine until she had made a hole. All the wine ran out

into the road. Then she did the same with each of the other casks, until all the wine was spilled.

At last the Carter looked round and discovered the empty casks.

"Alas, unlucky wretch that I am!" he cried.

"You shall be unluckier yet," chirped the Sparrow. She flew up between the horse's ears and pecked at him until he reared up in the shafts. The Carter drew out a hatchet and aimed a blow at the Sparrow. But she flew away, and the hatchet fell upon the horse's head and killed him.

"Alas, alas!" cried the Carter. "Unlucky wretch that I am!"

"Not wretch enough yet!" chirped the Sparrow. "Now I will plague and punish you at your house."

The Carter had to leave his cart by the roadside and walk home on foot, fuming with rage. The Sparrow flew on before him.

"Oh, wife!" he cried out when he entered his house. "Ill luck has come to me. My wine is all spilled and my horse is dead."

His wife ran to meet him with her apron thrown over her head. "Oh, husband!" she cried, "a little brown bird has flown into the loft where the corn is stored, and has brought with her all the birds in the world! They are eating up the corn as fast as they can."

The Carter ran up to the loft. It was just as his wife had said. A great flock of birds was devouring his corn, with the Sparrow in their midst.

"Alas, alas, alas!" he cried, "unlucky wretch that I am!"

"You shall be more unlucky and more wretched yet!" chirped the Sparrow. "Your cruelty shall cost you your life!"

The Carter went downstairs to the kitchen in a fine fury. He sat in the chimney corner, muttering angrily. Then the Sparrow came and perched on the

window sill. When the Carter saw her, he jumped up and seized his hatchet to strike at her. But the Sparrow flew away and his blow struck the window, which splintered into fragments. Now the Sparrow flew all round the house, hopping from place to place, and the Carter, mad with rage, ran after her with his hatchet. But she always flew away, and he only succeeded in breaking up all his furniture — the chairs, the table, the dishes, the glasses, and even the walls of his house. At last, however, he dropped the hatchet and managed to catch the Sparrow in his hands. She fluttered and beat her wings, but she could not escape.

"At last I have you!" shouted the Carter. He called his wife, and said: "Now, wife, take the hatchet, strike the bird, and kill her in my hand."

His wife picked up the hatchet and struck a blow with all her might. But she missed her aim and hit her husband on the head, so that he fell down dead.

And then the little brown Sparrow flew back to her nest in the hedgerow beside the high road.

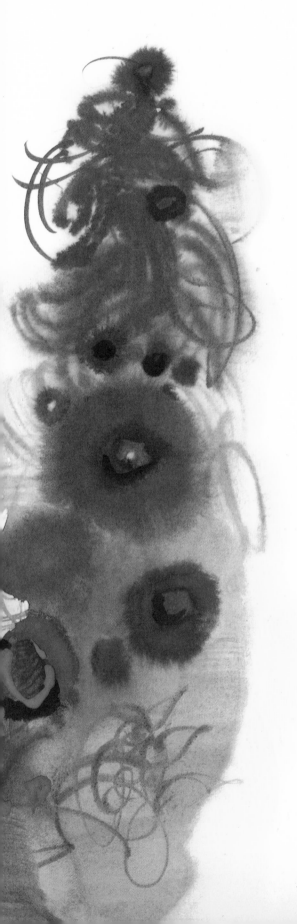

THE GREEDY DOG

A greedy Dog ran out from a butcher's shop, holding a juicy bone in her jaws.

The Butcher in his blue-and-white striped apron ran after the Dog, brandishing his sharp knife.

"Stop thief! Stop thief!" he cried.

But the Dog took no notice. She ran away as fast as she could, and soon she was quite out of sight and sound of the village. As she ran, she thought of the tasty meal she would soon enjoy.

"Just let me find a nice quiet place where no one will come to disturb me, and then I shall set to and eat up every scrap, marrow and all!" she thought greedily.

Presently the Dog reached a grassy water meadow with a wide stream flowing through it. Before she began her meal she decided to take a drink, for she had run a long way and felt hot. She went down to the edge of the stream, still holding the bone in her mouth. She was just about to lay it down on the grass in order to lap up some water when she saw another dog gazing up at her through the surface of the stream!

"Why, that dog staring up at me from the water is carrying a bone in his mouth too! And it looks as though it is a bigger and juicier bone than mine!"

And now the silly, greedy Dog was no longer content with that bone she had stolen. The other bone looked *much* bigger and *much* juicier. So she dropped the bone she was holding and made a sudden spring at the dog in the water, intending to snatch his bone from him.

Alas! Too late she realized that the other dog was merely her own reflection in the water. She clambered out of the stream, thoroughly wet and muddy, and saw her juicy bone being swept away by the current.

THE TIGER AND
THE HARE

Once, long ago, in a faraway country, there lived a Tiger. The other animals feared the Tiger, and ran away whenever they caught sight of his striped coat and yellow eyes as he came stalking through the jungle. But it happened one day that the Hare was caught by the Tiger before he had time to run away.

"Aha, little Hare!" said the Tiger. "Now I have caught you I am going to eat you up."

The Hare was very frightened, indeed. But he kept his wits about him.

"How glad I am to have met you, dear Uncle," he told the Tiger. "I have some delicious food that I have been keeping for you."

The Tiger was curious. He followed the Hare into the valley. Presently the Hare stopped beside a little heap of eleven smooth round pebbles. He picked one up and said: "Here we are, Uncle. Just try these – I'm sure you will find them quite delicious."

The Tiger looked at the pebbles with interest. "How do you eat them?" he asked.

"It's quite simple," answered the Hare. "You cook them in a fire until they turn red."

Then he lit a fire and put the pebbles in it. The Tiger watched them hungrily, eager to taste this new food. After a few moments, the Hare said: "I will go and fetch some bean sauce, Uncle. The pebbles will taste much better with bean sauce. I shall return directly. Mind you don't begin to eat while I am gone; there are only ten pebbles, and I would like five of them for myself!"

With that the Hare ran off. While the Tiger waited by the fire, he counted the pebbles. Already they had turned a deep red color. What do you think? He found there were eleven pebbles, not ten, as the Hare had said!

"If I take just one to try, it will never be missed," he thought to himself. Greedily he popped one of the red-hot pebbles into his mouth. Oh! how it scorched his tongue, his throat, his stomach! Howling with pain, the Tiger ran away to the hills.

And the little Hare, who had hidden nearby to watch all that happened, laughed and laughed at the success of his clever plan.

But a little while later, the Tiger came upon the Hare again. This time the Hare was crouching beside a leafy bush.

"Aha, little Hare! You shan't escape me this time," said the Tiger. "We have a score to settle, you and I."

The Hare trembled with fear. But still he kept his wits about him. "How lucky it is that you should come along just at this moment, Uncle!" he said. "Do you see what I am doing? I am chasing sparrows. If you look up toward the sky and keep your mouth wide open, I will drive them into it. What a feast you will have! It will be much better than the meal one little Hare could provide."

The Tiger saw that there were indeed a great many sparrows fluttering about the bush.

"Are you sure you are not trying to trick me again?" he asked suspiciously.

"Of course not, Uncle!" protested the Hare. "Just stand in the middle of the bush, look up at the sky, and open your mouth."

Well, the Tiger went into the middle of that leafy bush, and stood with his mouth wide open, gazing at the sky above. Then the Hare set fire to the bush. The crackling of the flames sounded like a thousand twittering sparrows.

"Watch out, Uncle, they are all coming your way!" he shouted. "Can you not hear them flying toward you?"

With that, the Hare ran off. The Tiger stood still in the midst of the burning bush. Soon he began to feel very hot – and suddenly he saw flames leaping all around him. With a roar he leaped to safety, but his striped coat was singed by the fire.

And the little Hare, who had hidden nearby, laughed and laughed.

A few weeks went by. Then the Tiger met the Hare a third time, on the bank of a deep rushing river.

"Aha, little Hare, we meet again!" he snarled. "Twice you have tricked me – but you shan't get away with it a third time! What have you to say for yourself before I open my jaws to eat you?"

The Hare twitched nervously, but still he kept his wits about him. "You misunderstand me, Uncle," he said in a humble voice. "I have only been trying to help you. It's not my fault that you burned your mouth with a red-hot pebble, and singed your coat in the burning bush." Then he gave the Tiger a sly look. "How would you like a feast of fish, Uncle? There are hundreds of fish in this deep rushing river."

The Tiger was interested to hear about the fish. "Well little Hare," he said, "this is your third and last chance. Mind you don't try to trick me again! – How do you catch these fish?"

"Trust me, Uncle," answered the Hare. "Now all you have to do is to lean down over the water and scoop them up with your great big paw."

"That seems easy enough," said the Tiger greedily.

He went to the very brink of the river and leaned down low over the water. At once the Hare leaped forward and gave the Tiger's long striped tail such a tweak that he toppled and fell right into that deep rushing river and was drowned. And that was the third and last time the Hare met the Tiger.

THE TOMTIT AND THE BEAR

One summer's day a gray Wolf and a brown Bear were walking through a wood. High in a tree a bird sang so delightfully that the Bear said:

"Listen to that song, brother Wolf! What bird can it be that sings so wonderfully?"

"Do you not know?" replied the Wolf, "that that is the King of the birds. We should all show the respect due to his majesty."

Although the Bear did not know it, the Wolf was talking nonsense. The bird singing in the tree was only an ordinary tomtit.

"I would very much like to see the King's palace," said the Bear. "Do show me where it is."

"If you really want to see it," the Wolf told him, "we shall have to wait until the Queen comes home."

In a little while the mother Tomtit flew back to her nest, carrying in her beak a juicy tidbit. The father Tomtit joined her, and together they fed their little ones in the nest.

"Now let us go to look at the palace!" cried the Bear eagerly.

But the Wolf restrained him. "No, no, we must wait until another day, when the King and Queen are not at home. It would not do to disturb their majesties now."

How the Bear longed to see the royal palace of the King and Queen of the birds! The very next day he came back to the bush where the tomtits had built their nest, and waited until he saw the King and Queen fly away. Then he went over to the bush and peered inside. How disappointed he was! He saw only an ordinary bird's nest, with five or six little birds inside it!

"This is no royal palace!" exclaimed the Bear in disgust. "It is nothing but a wretched, dirty bundle of twigs. And as for these little birds, they are no princes or princesses, but ordinary brats!"

At this, the young tomtits began to chatter

and chirp angrily. "How dare you call us such names, you stupid old Bear!" they screamed. "We'll see that you are punished for your insults!"

The Bear was frightened by this threat and went home to his den. Presently the mother and father tomtits came back to their nest, but the little tomtits refused to eat the food they had brought in their beaks. "We will not touch one morsel until that wicked Bear is punished for insulting us!" they said.

"He shall be punished all right, never fear," their father promised.

He flew off at once to the Bear's den. "Bruin the Bear!" he called. "Listen to me! You have shamefully insulted my children. We therefore declare war upon you!"

When the Bear heard this, he summoned all the four-footed creatures to help him fight the war: the Ox, the Ass, the Stag, and every other animal the earth contains. And the Tomtit enlisted on his side every creature that flies in the air: all the birds, both great and small, and all the insects, including the Hornet, the Gnat and the Bee.

Before the battle began, the Tomtit sent out spies to discover who was the enemy's Commander-in-Chief. The Gnat was the most successful spy. As dusk was falling, she found out where the Bear and his allies were gathered in the wood, and hid herself under a tree leaf to listen to their plans. She heard the Bear say to the red-brown Fox:

"Reynard, you are the most cunning creature of us all. You shall be our Commander-in-Chief and lead us into battle. We must arrange a signal so that we shall know what you want us to do. What shall it be?"

The Fox replied: "I have a fine red bushy tail. When you see me carry it high in the air, you may be sure the battle is won, and you must advance on the enemy. But if you see me drop my tail between my legs, then the day is lost, and you must retreat immediately."

All this was overheard by the Gnat. She flew back to the Tomtit and reported the enemy's plans.

The next morning, at first light, both sides drew up in battle array. The Bear and all the four-footed creatures, with the red-brown Fox at their head, charged forward with such a mighty noise that the earth trembled. The Tomtit and all the creatures of the air came flying toward them, humming and buzzing so that the sky was filled with the sound of their anger.

Now the Tomtit ordered the Hornet to attack the Fox by stinging his tail. The Hornet advanced on the enemy Commander-in-Chief, fastened himself onto the fine red bushy tail held so proudly on high, and stung as hard as he could. When the Fox felt the first sting, as sharp as a red-hot needle, he drew one leg up in pain, but bravely kept his tail upright. When he felt the second sting, he could not help lowering his tail for a moment. But when he felt the third sting, he could bear it no longer, and turned and fled with his tail between his legs.

When the other animals saw this, they cried out: "Alas, the day is lost! Retreat! Retreat!"

And they too fled from the field of battle, leaving the Tomtit and his forces victorious.

Then the Tomtit flew back to his nest. "Rejoice, children, for we have won the war!" he chirped. "Now eat the food your mother and I brought for you."

But the little ones replied: "All is not yet finished. Before we eat, that villainous Bear must come to the nest to humbly ask our pardon for calling us brats."

So the Tomtit flew to the Bear's den once again.

"Bruin!" he called, "you are to come to my nest to humbly ask pardon of my children for calling them brats."

The Bear was in a great sulk. Nevertheless, he crept out from his den and did as the Tomtit bade him. And now at last the young tomtits were satisfied, and ate their fill of the good things their parents had brought.

THE FOOLISH ASS

An Ass was crossing a narrow footbridge that led across a fast-flowing river. His sides were heavily burdened, and his master goaded him on with a stick.

The Ass laid back his long ears and brayed fearfully. He was sure he would fall into the water. Sure enough, with the next step he took he lost his footing and tumbled into the river, burdens and all.

"Now I'm done for!" he thought. "If it weren't for these burdens on my back, I could save my life by swimming to the opposite bank."

But the Ass was lucky. He was carrying a load of salt and, when he fell into the water, the salt dissolved. So he was able to swim to dry land unhampered by his burdens after all.

Not long after this, he made the same journey. Once again he carried a double pack on his back and, when he reached the river, his master began to urge him along the narrow footbridge as he had done before.

"Aha!" thought the Ass. "This time I know better. Why should I trouble to keep my balance along this bridge? If I let myself fall into the water, my burdens will vanish as they did before. I would indeed be a fool to continue the rest of this journey loaded, when I can so easily get rid of my packs!"

And so he let himself fall with a mighty *splash* into the water.

But alas! He would have been wiser to keep to the footbridge after all. For this time he was carrying a load of sponges, and when he fell into the river they grew so heavy that the Ass could not keep his head above water, and was drowned.

THE UNGRATEFUL TIGER

The hunter in the jungle dug deep pits to trap the animals who lived there and one day he trapped a mighty Tiger. The Tiger howled in despair, for he knew that soon the hunter would come with his sharp spear.

He had not been there long, however, before a Traveler passed by. The Traveler took pity on the Tiger. He picked up a fallen branch from the ground and put one end down into the pit so that the Tiger could crawl out.

But no sooner was the Tiger out of the pit than he turned on the Traveler and showed his teeth. "I am hungry and I am going to eat you up!" he snarled.

"You wicked creature!" cried the Traveler. "How could you do such a thing after I have just rescued you from the pit, and from the spear of the hunter? You owe me a debt of gratitude!"

"There is no such thing as a debt of gratitude," answered the Tiger. "All I know is that I am hungry and that you will provide me with a satisfying meal."

"Let us find a judge who will decide on this matter," begged the Traveler.

"Very well," the Tiger agreed. "I will abide by a judge's decision."

So they went into the forest in search of a judge, and on the way they came upon the Skull of an ox.

"This Skull looks wise," said the Traveler. "Let us ask it to judge our case."

"As you like," said the Tiger.

The Skull listened attentively to the arguments put forward by the Traveler and the Tiger, then gave its decision.

"The Tiger is right. There is no such thing as a debt of gratitude. I should know! For years I served my master faithfully, yoked to his plow. Then I grew old. What happened? Was my master grateful for the years of service I had given him? No!

He killed and ate me. So the Tiger should eat the Traveler."

"I will eat you now!" roared the Tiger.

The Traveler, however, claimed the right of appeal to a second judge.

"Very well," grumbled the Tiger. "I know the law. But I am getting very hungry indeed!"

Presently they came to the Banyan Tree, and stood beneath its spreading branches. The Banyan Tree was known to be one of the wisest trees in the jungle.

"Let us ask the Banyan Tree to decide our dispute," said the Traveler.

"By all means," agreed the Tiger.

So they put their case before the Banyan Tree. And when the Banyan Tree had heard both sides of the argument, it said: "In my opinion, the Tiger is right. There is no such thing as a debt of gratitude. Look at me. People come to rest under my shady branches from the heat of the sun, and to shelter from the rain. Yet in return they break my branches and steal my flowers. So the Tiger should eat the Traveler."

"I will eat you now!" roared the Tiger.

But the Traveler claimed the right of appeal to a third judge.

"This is your last chance," the Tiger told him. "We may go before three judges only with the same dispute. That is the law."

They had not gone very far before they met the Rabbit.

"Wise Rabbit," said the Traveler, "please settle our difference of opinion."

The Rabbit heard all they had to say. Then, looking very wise, he said: "I cannot possibly pass judgment in this case until I have visited the scene of the dispute."

So the Traveler and the Tiger led the Rabbit back to the hunter's pit.

"Now," said the Rabbit, "let me see exactly where you were, Tiger, when the Traveler came to rescue you."

The Tiger jumped down into the pit. "I was down here, right at the bottom, just like this!" he called.

Then the Traveler removed the branch from the pit. "Of course, this branch wasn't in the pit when I first saw the Tiger," he explained to the Rabbit.

The Rabbit turned to the Traveler with a smile. "Now you had best be on your way," he said, "And if you will take my advice, you won't help such a thankless creature in future!" Then he looked down at the Tiger. "As for you, ungrateful wretch, you can stay where you are!"

"How wise you are, Rabbit!" the Traveler cried as he set off along his road.

The Rabbit returned to his burrow. The Tiger in the pit roared with fury, but he roared in vain, for no one else rescued him.

73

THE COYOTE AND
THE TURTLE

One fine morning a young Turtle crawled out of the cool, deep river where he had lived for as long as he could remember. He wanted to explore the big wide world. He crawled farther and farther away from his river home, toward the hot dry desert where the cactus and the prickly pear grew. What a foolish young Turtle he was! He did not realize that the hot, strong sun was bad for him. River turtles should stay near the cool water. They soon die in the hot sunshine.

As the day wore on, the sun rose in the sky and blazed down upon the hot dry desert. It did not take the little Turtle long to discover his mistake. He turned around and began to crawl back to his home. But

the river was a long way away by now, and soon he could go no farther. He crawled under a spiky gray-green cactus plant to try to seek some shade. He was afraid he would never get home, and he began to cry bitterly.

In a little while, along came a Coyote. Coyotes are the desert wolves, cunning and cruel. Their coats are the color of the desert sand. This Coyote heard the little Turtle crying under the cactus plant.

"That is a fine song the Turtle sings!" he thought. "I would like him to teach it to me."

So he asked the little Turtle to teach him his song.

"But I am not singing, Mr. Coyote," sobbed the Turtle. "Indeed I am not. I have never felt less like singing in my life."

The Coyote did not believe him. He thought the little Turtle wanted to keep his song a secret. He snarled, showing his sharp teeth.

"If you do not teach me your song, little Turtle, I will swallow you for my dinner!"

Now, although the little Turtle had been so foolish as to leave his cool damp home in the river and venture into the hot dry desert, in other ways he was wise, like all his kind. And now he kept his wits about him.

"You would not enjoy your dinner, Mr. Coyote," he said. "Indeed, you would not. My hard shell would stick in your throat when you tried to swallow me."

The Coyote looked at the Turtle's hard shell, and saw that this was true. "In that case, little Turtle, I will take you out of the shade of the cactus plant and throw you into the hot sunshine," he said, smiling cruelly.

The little Turtle was very frightened. However, he said bravely: "That would not hurt me, Mr. Coyote, for I would draw my head and my four feet right under my shell, out of the hot sunshine."

Of course, the little Turtle would not really be able to protect himself by doing this, but luckily for him the Coyote believed his words. He thought again. "I know what I shall do with you, little Turtle!" he said at last. "Because you will not teach me your song, I will punish you by throwing you into the cold, deep river."

How the little Turtle smiled to himself! But he did not let the Coyote see how pleased he was. Oh, no – he pretended to be very frightened, indeed.

"Oh, Mr. Coyote, don't do that! Don't throw me into the river! I would drown in the cold, deep water! Indeed, I would!"

"I *will* throw you into the river!" snarled the Coyote – and then he seized the little Turtle in his mouth, and carried him all the way back to the river, where he threw him *splash* into the water.

How cool and damp it was! How much better than the hot dry desert! The little Turtle swam happily into the middle of the river, where the Coyote could not reach him, and called cheerfully: "Thank you, Mr. Coyote! Thank you for bringing me home! I'm very grateful for your help, indeed, I am!"

And when the Coyote realized how he had been tricked by the little Turtle, he barked angrily and loped off into the sunshine.

DIVIDING THE CHEESE

Once upon a time, two thieving Cats stole a big yellow cheese.

"Let us divide the cheese," said the first Cat. He was a fine fellow with a striped coat and long whiskers. "I will share it out between the two of us."

"Not so fast, my friend," said the second Cat. He was jet black, except for one white paw, and he had a cauliflower ear.

"What is the matter?" asked the first Cat.

"How can I be sure that you will divide the cheese equally?" said the second Cat. "You may decide to give more to yourself than to me. I think we should get a third person to divide it for us."

"Very well," agreed the first Cat. "But I'm sorry to see you don't trust me, my friend."

So the black Cat and the stripy Cat looked around for a third person whom they could ask to divide the big yellow cheese for them. They soon found a bright-eyed Monkey, who had been sitting in a banana tree overhead, and had overheard their conversation.

"Please, Monkey, be so good as to divide this cheese into two equal parts," the Cats begged him.

The Monkey smiled to himself, for he thought he could turn this request to his own advantage. "Wait here while I fetch a cheese-cutter and a scale," he told them. "I shall have to weigh each piece to make sure they are equal."

In another moment he returned with a wire cheese-cutter and a balancing-scale. He cut the big yellow cheese in two pieces, while the stripy Cat and the black Cat watched anxiously. But the Monkey cut one piece larger than the other, and so when he put each piece on either side of the balancing-scale, of course the one weighed heavier than the other.

"Oh dear," said the Monkey. "I didn't

the other piece,'' he said. ''You do want me to be absolutely fair, don't you?''

''Oh yes, of course,'' replied the Cats doubtfully. And they watched even more anxiously as Monkey weighed the two bits of cheese again. But alas! He had taken a little too much of the larger piece, which now weighed lighter than the other bit.

Monkey shook his head. ''Dear me,'' he said, ''I ate rather too much, didn't I? Never mind, I'll soon correct that!'' And he crossed over and began to eat the other piece of cheese.

''Look here, Monkey,'' protested the Cats, ''we didn't invite you here to enjoy a feast, you know!''

Monkey's face assumed a very innocent expression.

''I'm only trying to be quite fair,'' he said in a hurt voice. ''You did ask me to divide this cheese equally. I'm doing my best!''

Now he weighed the two pieces of cheese a third time. By now, both pieces had become quite small, Still they did not balance evenly on the scale, and Monkey again began to eat from the heavier piece.

At this, the two Cats could sit by and watch him eating that delicious cheese no longer.

''Stop, stop!'' they cried, ''let us have what is left, for pity's sake!''

The Monkey now saw that the game was up. ''Oh, very well,'' he said, ''take your cheese. I see you are not really interested in having fair shares at all. You are just a couple of greedy old thieves!''

And he sprang back into the banana tree, and began to pelt the two Cats with little green bananas.

The black Cat and the stripy Cat each pounced upon a piece of cheese. They no longer cared whether one piece was bigger than the other or not! But by this time, both pieces were so small that I am afraid they were only able to swallow a few crumbs. You see, the bright-eyed Monkey had eaten by far the larger part of that big yellow cheese.

divide it very well, did I? I shall have to even things up.''

And then he began to eat the heavier piece of cheese.

''Hey, Monkey, what d'you think you're doing?'' the Cats demanded indignantly.

Monkey looked at them in surprise. ''Why, I'm making this heavy piece of cheese lighter, so that it will balance with

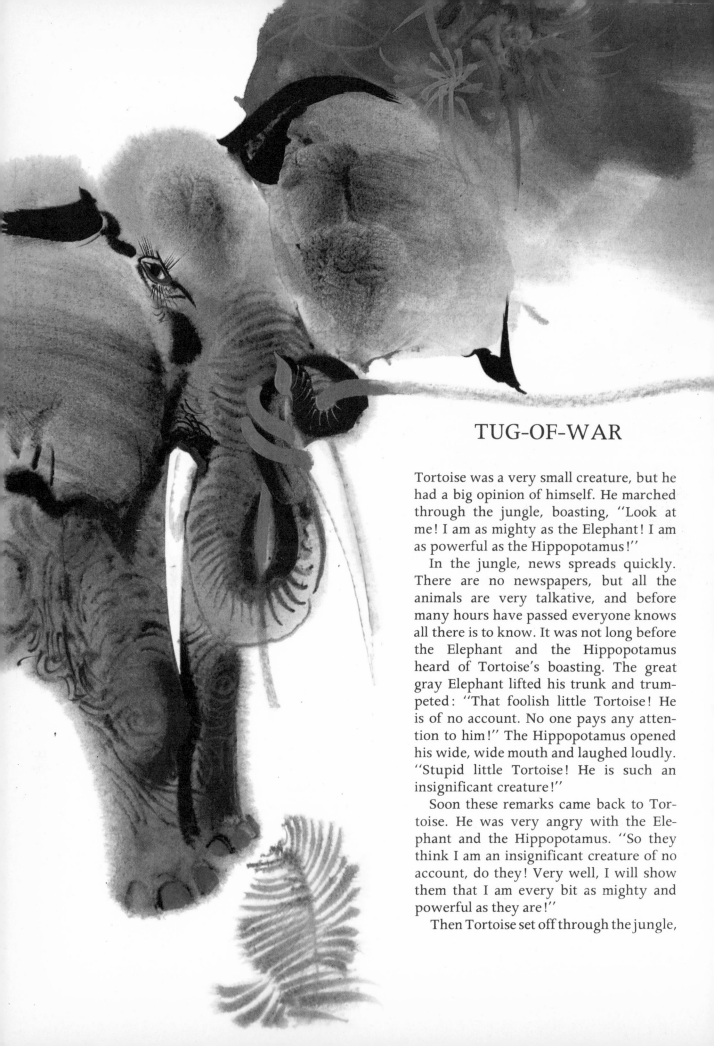

TUG-OF-WAR

Tortoise was a very small creature, but he had a big opinion of himself. He marched through the jungle, boasting, "Look at me! I am as mighty as the Elephant! I am as powerful as the Hippopotamus!"

In the jungle, news spreads quickly. There are no newspapers, but all the animals are very talkative, and before many hours have passed everyone knows all there is to know. It was not long before the Elephant and the Hippopotamus heard of Tortoise's boasting. The great gray Elephant lifted his trunk and trumpeted: "That foolish little Tortoise! He is of no account. No one pays any attention to him!" The Hippopotamus opened his wide, wide mouth and laughed loudly. "Stupid little Tortoise! He is such an insignificant creature!"

Soon these remarks came back to Tortoise. He was very angry with the Elephant and the Hippopotamus. "So they think I am an insignificant creature of no account, do they! Very well, I will show them that I am every bit as mighty and powerful as they are!"

Then Tortoise set off through the jungle,

until he came to the place where the great gray Elephant lay in the shade of a banana tree. What a mighty animal the Elephant was, with his long trunk, his strong tusks, and his enormous feet! The little Tortoise crept right up to him and cried:

"Ho, Elephant, here I am! Get up and greet me as your friend!"

The Elephant turned his head to see who had addressed him in such a familiar way. He was astonished when he saw the little Tortoise. "How dare you call me Friend, small person?" he asked indignantly.

"I call you Friend because we are equal in strength and power," replied the Tortoise. "You think this cannot be so, because you are large and I am small. But you are wrong. I will prove it! Let us hold a tug-of-war!"

"That is a very silly suggestion, little Tortoise," replied the Elephant.

"I am willing to pull against you, if you are willing to pull against me," the Tortoise told him. "Whichever of us succeeds in pulling over the other shall prove himself the greater. But if neither of us succeeds, then we are equal, and we will call each other Friend."

The Elephant sighed. "Oh, very well, little Tortoise, I will pull against you," he agreed.

Then the Tortoise cut a very long vine, and carried one end of it to the Elephant. "This end is yours," he said. "I will walk off with my end to a distant spot. Then we must tug against each other until one of us pulls over the other, or the vine breaks in two."

The Tortoise walked slowly out of sight, carrying one end of the vine in his mouth. He walked as far as the oozy river, where he found the Hippopotamus wallowing in the mud.

"Ho, Hippopotamus!" he shouted,

79

"here I am! Get up and greet me as your friend!"

The Hippopotamus looked up to see who was shouting at him in such an insolent manner. He was amazed when he saw the little Tortoise. "How dare you call me Friend, small person?" he asked indignantly.

"I call you Friend because we are equal in strength and power," replied the Tortoise. "You think this cannot be so, because you are large and I am small. But you are wrong. I will prove it! Let us hold a tug-of-war."

"That is an extremely foolish notion, little Tortoise," replied the Hippopotamus.

"I am willing to pull against you, if you are willing to pull against me," the Tortoise told him.

And at last the Hippopotamus agreed to take part in the tug-of-war, just as the Elephant had before him. Then the Tortoise gave the Hippopotamus the end of

the vine which he held in his mouth. "This end is yours," he told him. "I will go away and pick up the other end. Then we must tug against each other until one of us pulls over the other, or the vine breaks in two."

Now you can see the clever plan that was in Tortoise's head. There was Elephant, holding one end of the vine, and here was Hippopotamus, holding the other end! Tortoise went to the middle of the vine, out of sight of both and pinched it hard.

As soon as the Elephant and Hippopotamus felt the vine move, they each began to pull on it as hard as they could. How Elephant heaved and grunted! How Hippopotamus puffed and puffed! The vine was stretched taut, and neither could pull over the other, but still they kept on tugging.

"Oh mighty little Tortoise!" groaned the great Elephant.

"Oh powerful small person!" exclaimed

the Hippopotamus, pulling even harder.

Tortoise watched the quivering vine, and then he went off to enjoy a feast of mushrooms, leaving the Elephant and the Hippopotamus still pulling hard. He finished his mushrooms, then took a little nap. When he woke up it was sunset.

"I had better go back to see how those two are getting on," he thought to himself.

He came back to the middle of the vine. It was still stretched taut. Elephant and Hippopotamus had tugged against each other all day long, but neither had yet succeeded in pulling over the other!

"This has gone on long enough," Tortoise said; and he bit the vine in two.

What do you think happened? When the vine went slack, Elephant and Hippopotamus both fell over backwards onto the ground. Two tremendous *thumps*

echoed loudly through the hot jungle.

Now Tortoise crawled off to see Elephant.

"Oh, Tortoise," Elephant said, "I did not realize how strong you are. The vine broke, so we are equals. You were right – size is not everything. We will call each other Friend."

Tortoise was jubilant. He had triumphed over the great gray Elephant! Now he crawled off to see Hippopotamus.

"Oh, Tortoise," Hippopotamus said, "I had no idea you were so strong. The vine broke, so we are equals. You were right – size is not everything."

How pleased Tortoise was! He had triumphed over the Hippopotamus as well.

And from that day forward, whenever the little Tortoise met the mighty Elephant or the powerful Hippopotamus as he went about the jungle, they called him Friend.

THE FOX AND THE LION IN PARTNERSHIP

Once upon a time it happened that a Lion fell sick. He could no longer stalk his prey across the plains and through the forest. He lay in a cave all day long, and in order to get his food he was forced to resort to cunning. He decided to go into partnership with the red-brown Fox; for what creature is more crafty than the Fox? And for his part, the Fox was glad enough to become the Lion's comrade.

"If you would like to see me recover," the Lion told his new partner, "you must use your quick wits and flattering tongue to entice the other animals within reach of my claws." He licked his lips. "I would like to get my teeth into the tender flesh of the big Deer that lives in the forest. Go and see if you can persuade him to come here, my friend."

The Fox trotted off into the forest, and presently he came upon the big Deer playing in a sunlit glade. The Fox spoke to the Deer with honeyed words.

"I bring you good news, brother. As you may have heard, our king the Lion is very ill. Alas, he will soon be dead. Before he dies, however, he wants to appoint one of the other animals to reign after him. He has considered each animal in turn – the pig thinks of nothing except filling his belly; the bear is a lazy good-for-nothing; the leopard is bad-tempered; the tiger is vain and boastful. But you, brother Deer, seem well qualified to take the Lion's place. You are tall and stately, you live long, and your antlers are a good defense against your enemies. Yes, the Lion would like you to succeed him as king."

The Deer listened carefully to the Fox's speech, and his mind became puffed up with pride. He was to be king of all the animals! The Lion had chosen him to rule in his place!

"The Lion has paid me a great honour, brother Fox," said the Deer. "And indeed, all that you say about my stately bearing, my strong antlers, and my long life is true. I

shall reign well over my fellow creatures. I will be a good king."

The Fox smiled craftily. "If you will take my advice, I think you should come back with me now to the Lion's cave. He is waiting to know whether you will agree to accept the nomination."

The Deer followed the Fox through the forest back to the Lion's cave, without any suspicion of what lay in wait for him. Sure enough, there the sick Lion lay, his great head resting on his paws. When he saw the red-brown Fox returning with the Deer, his eyes glinted with pleasure. As soon as the Deer came within reach, he pounced upon him eagerly – but he only succeeded in tearing his ears. The Deer escaped from the Lion's grasp, and fled back to the forest.

The Fox beat his paws together in disappointment, and the Lion growled and groaned. He begged the Fox to try to entice the Deer to the cave again.

"And this time he shall not escape me!" the Lion promised. "Oh, how hungry I am!"

The Fox waved his bushy tail. "It will be a difficult task to perform, dear friend. But for your sake I will attempt it."

So he set off once more. It was easy enough to follow the tracks of the Deer, for they were spotted with blood from the wound the Lion had inflicted on him. Before long the Fox found the Deer resting beneath a tall tree.

The Deer was furious when he saw the Fox. "I wonder how you dare to show your face again!" he said angrily. "You can't trick me a second time. You'd better go and

spin your story to some other creature who would like to be king. Be off with you – or I'll charge you with my antlers!"

The Fox looked at the Deer slyly. "How suspicious you are, brother Deer. And how nervously you behaved in the presence of the Lion. I assure you that he is filled with benevolence toward you. He wishes you nothing but good. When he caught hold of your ears, he only meant to whisper some secrets of kingship. If he gave you a little scratch by mistake – why, that was only because he does not realize his own strength."

The Deer considered the Fox's words. Could what he said be true? Perhaps he had acted foolishly in the presence of the Lion.

"If you really do want to be king," the Fox continued, pressing his advantage, "I advise you to return with me to the Lion's cave at once, and tell him how sorry you are that you behaved so badly. He is very angry about it, and is talking of choosing the Wolf to reign after him instead. Make haste! Follow me, and go up to him without fear. He won't hurt you, I swear it!"

Once more the Deer was persuaded. Meekly he followed the Fox back to the cave.

The Lion was overjoyed when he saw the Fox returning with the Deer a second time.

"How wise of me to form a partnership with such a crafty creature!" he thought.

As soon as the Deer entered the cave, the Lion fell upon him and swallowed his flesh and bones. The Fox looked on, as pleased as the Lion at the success of his mission. As the Lion ate his meal, the Fox seized upon the brains and gulped them down, for he was hungry, too. The Lion noticed they were missing and began looking for them among the leftovers.

"You might as well stop looking," the Fox told him. "The simple truth is that the Deer had no brains. Well – I ask you – would you expect a creature with any brains at all to come twice into a Lion's den?"

OLD MAN CROCODILE

Old man Crocodile lay in the shallow, muddy river, under the noonday sun. A Carrion Crow alighted on a branch of a tree that grew beside the river. He looked at old man Crocodile, and his mouth watered. "What a wonderful feast I and all my relatives would enjoy if only I could kill the Crocodile!" he thought.

"Ho, there, old man Crocodile!" he called. "What a stick-in-the-mud you are! Why do you stay in this shallow river all the time? Don't you know there is a much deeper river only a short distance from here?"

Old man Crocodile opened one eyelid. "I have never heard of such a river," he grunted sleepily.

"I am only telling you the truth," said the cunning Crow. "I want to help you."

Old man Crocodile opened his other eyelid. "Hm, I would like to see this other river. Will you show me the way, Master Crow?"

"Oh yes, I'll show you the way," replied the Crow. "It isn't far; I'm sure a big, strong creature like yourself will easily be able to walk there."

So old man Crocodile heaved himself on to the river bank. The Crow spread his glossy back feathers and flew ahead of him. Slowly the Crocodile followed the Crow. Foolish Crocodile! He should not have strayed onto the land. Crocodiles cannot survive for long once they leave the cool rivers where they make their homes. After they had been traveling a mile or so, he began to groan.

"We have come a long way, Master Crow. Is it much farther to your river?"

"We are nearly there," replied the Crow. "Surely a big strong creature like yourself cannot be feeling tired already?"

The Crocodile felt ashamed of his tiredness. He stumbled on, still following the Crow. But at last he could go no farther; he collapsed and lay helpless on the ground.

"I cannot go on, Master Crow; I am quite exhausted!" he moaned.

The Crow flew above old man Crocodile's head, laughing and mocking at him. "What a stupid Crocodile you are! You should have stayed at home. There is no other river! You will soon die here from starvation and thirst. Then I will come and eat you up!" And he flew away to tell all his relations to prepare themselves for a wonderful feast of crocodile meat.

Presently, however, a kind-hearted villager came upon the scene, driving a bullock cart. The Crocodile begged him to save his life and take him back to his river.

"Please help me!" he cried.

The villager felt sorry for old man Crocodile. But he knew that crocodiles are not to be trusted. So before he put him in the cart, he bound his jaws together with a strong rope. Then he drove his cart back to the shallow muddy river, took the Crocodile out of the cart, and laid him on the bank.

"Kind master," said the Crocodile, "I am so weak after my unfortunate experience that I have not strength enough to crawl into the water. Please drive your cart into the river and drop me there."

The villager thought there could be no

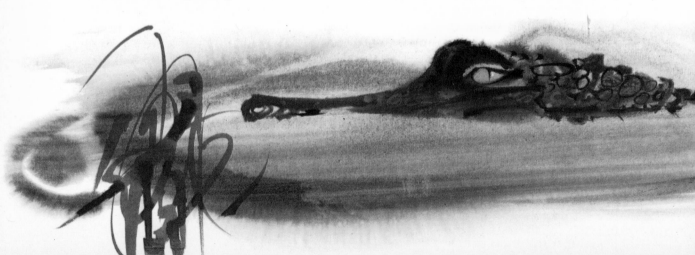

harm in this, so he whipped up the bullocks and drove his cart into the river, where he untied the Crocodile's jaws and pushed him into the water. At once that wicked old man Crocodile opened his jaws wide and caught hold of one of the bullock's legs with his sharp teeth.

"Let go, you ungrateful creature!" cried the villager.

But old man Crocodile took no notice, for he was very hungry.

At that moment, a Rabbit came down to the river to drink. He saw what was happening, and shouted: "Hit the Crocodile with your driving stick! Hit him hard!"

The villager did as he was told. He hit the Crocodile so hard that he let go of the bullock. Then he drove his cart back to the bank and thanked the Rabbit for his good advice.

Old man Crocodile was very angry. "But for that interfering Rabbit," he said to himself, "I would have enjoyed a good meal of bullock." He decided to catch the Rabbit, and watched and waited for him to come again to the river to drink.

The Rabbit came to the river the very next day. Old man Crocodile lurked at the river's edge. But the water was so shallow that only his head and tail were submerged; his back remained exposed. He stayed quite still, hoping the Rabbit would mistake him for a log. But the Rabbit was wise; he looked at the strange log in the water and said aloud: "If that were really a log, it would float downstream."

At once the Crocodile swam a little way downstream, just to convince the Rabbit that he was indeed a log. The Rabbit seized his opportunity and drank quickly while the Crocodile was out of the way.

"You can't catch me, old man Crocodile!" he shouted as he scampered back home.

The Crocodile was furious. "We'll see about that!" he said.

The next day, he lurked once more by the river's edge and waited for the Rabbit. Once again the Rabbit saw the Crocodile's back above the water, and said aloud: "If that were really a log, it would float downstream."

This time the Crocodile stayed perfectly still.

"It must be a log after all!" the Rabbit thought to himself; and he put down his little head to drink.

Snap! Old man Crocodile caught hold of the Rabbit in his cruel jaws. He did not eat him at once, however. He wanted all the other animals to know how clever he had been to outwit the wise Rabbit. He swam up and down the river, laughing and shouting with glee. "Hee, hee, hee! Clever me! Hee, hee, hee! Clever me!"

Even though he was inside the Crocodile's mouth, the Rabbit kept his wits about him. "You stupid old Crocodile," he cried scornfully. "We all know you can shout 'hee, hee, hee.' Anyone can do that. But can you shout 'ha, ha, ha'?"

"Of course I can!" the Crocodile replied indignantly. "Ha, ha, ha!"

But in order to shout "ha, ha, ha," he had to open his jaw as wide as he could. In a flash the Rabbit jumped out of his mouth and was soon safely on dry land once more.

How angry old man Crocodile was! He thrashed his tail and wept big crocodile tears of rage. But he never had another opportunity to catch the clever little Rabbit.

MONKEY, CHIPMUNK AND CROCODILE

A teakwood tree stood in the middle of the forest. Hanging from one of its branches was a large, oval wild bees' nest. Along the forest path came Monkey. When he saw the wild bees' nest, it gave him an idea.

"I will play a trick on Chipmunk!" he said to himself. "It will serve him right for always thinking he knows more than anyone else."

Then Monkey went to look for Chipmunk. He found him sitting on the ground below the tree where he lived, nibbling a nut which he held in his two forepaws.

"Hello, Chipmunk," he greeted him. "Do you know what I have just seen? There is a big gong hanging from one of the branches of the teakwood tree that stands in the middle of the forest. I would like to make some music, but I don't know how to beat a gong. You are so clever that I thought you could teach me."

Chipmunk didn't really know how to make gong music either, but he didn't tell Monkey this. Instead, he said: "Of course I can teach you how to beat the gong, Monkey. Just show me where it is."

So Monkey led Chipmunk to the teak-

wood tree in the middle of the forest. "There it is!" he cried, pointing to the wild bees' nest.

Chipmunk at once began to climb the tree. Monkey retreated to a safe distance to watch what would happen. When Chipmunk got near the bees' nest, he heard a loud humming and buzzing from inside it.

"Ho, Monkey!" he called, "there is certainly plenty of music inside this gong. Just wait till I strike it!"

"Go ahead, Chipmunk!" Monkey shouted. "I'm watching carefully to see what you do."

Then Chipmunk began to beat the bees' nest as hard as he could: *wham, wham, wham!*

All at once, a great cloud of angry bees swarmed out of the nest, buzzing so loudly that they drowned the noise of Chipmunk's cries for help. How those bees stung Chipmunk! How he howled with pain and rage when he realized the trick Monkey had played on him! He came rushing down the tree as fast as he could, his bushy tail stretched out behind him. As for Monkey, he laughed till the tears ran down his cheeks. "You're not so clever after all, my friend!" he mocked. "Fancy mistaking a bees' nest for a gong! Silly old Chipmunk! Foolish old Chipmunk!"

Chipmunk did not forget this trick that

had been played on him. When he had recovered from all the bees' stings, he made
up his mind that he would seek his
revenge on Monkey. One fine day, he
sought out Monkey in the forest and said:
"How would you like to come with me to
the beach, my friend, and see if we can
find some shellfish to eat? They would
make a pleasant change from bananas and
mangoes."

Monkey thought this was a good idea,
and agreed to go along with Chipmunk.
When they got to the beach it was low
tide, and there were plenty of mussels and
sea-snails lying in the dry sand. They
cracked open the shells, and made a good
meal.

Suddenly Chipmunk caught sight of a
very big mollusk, a special sort of shellfish,
which had been left high and dry by the
receding tide. As soon as he saw it, he
smiled to himself, for he knew that here
was the means whereby he could pay
Monkey back for the trick he had played
on him with the bees.

"Here, Monkey, come quickly!" he
cried, "Look what I've found!"

Monkey came running to see what Chipmunk was making such a fuss about. He
was very impressed when he saw the size
of the mollusk.

"There's enough inside this shell to
provide a feast for both of us," Chipmunk
told him. Then he went on: "Your arm is
longer than mine, Monkey. You reach
down into the shell to take the creature
out."

Without stopping to think, Monkey
reached inside the gigantic shell with one
of his long arms. But as soon as his hand
touched the creature inside, the two
halves of the huge shell snapped together,
for that is the way of mollusks. Monkey
was well and truly trapped!

He yelled with pain, pulling and tugging
to get free, but it was no use. He could not
free himself.

"Help, help!" he cried. "I'm trapped!"

"Surely you don't expect me to help you?" said the Chipmunk. "Have you forgotten all about the bees' nest? Now you know what I felt like when I was stung so badly!"

And with that, Chipmunk ran off.

Well, Monkey just had to stay where he was, with his arm trapped inside the mollusk, until the tide came in, and the great shellfish opened up again. Then, groaning with pain, he limped slowly back to the forest.

It so happened that old man Crocodile was basking on the beach. When he saw Monkey limping along, he thought: "There's an easy catch for me! A fine tasty monkey for my supper – scrumptious!"

And he began to follow Monkey into the forest. Monkey was terribly frightened. He could not hurry, and soon old man Crocodile was snapping at his heels. At last Monkey reached an oak tree that stood on the edge of the forest. He grabbed a low-hanging branch and swung himself up – but alas! the Crocodile caught hold of Monkey's tail in his cruel jaws.

Monkey kept his wits about him. "You silly old Crocodile!" he cried scornfully. "You think you've caught hold of my tail, don't you! But really it's the root of this oak tree that you've got in your mouth. I don't know why you keep on chewing it – it must taste awful! I'm surprised you made such a stupid mistake; I thought Crocodiles were clever creatures."

When old man Crocodile heard Monkey's words, he spat out the tail at once, just to show how clever he really was. Monkey at once leaped to the very top of the tree, and called out:

"You are twice a fool, old man Crocodile! To think you had hold of my tail all the time, and then let it go! Now I know that Crocodiles are stupid creatures."

Old man Crocodile went off grumbling, and Monkey made his way across the tree-tops into the heart of the forest.

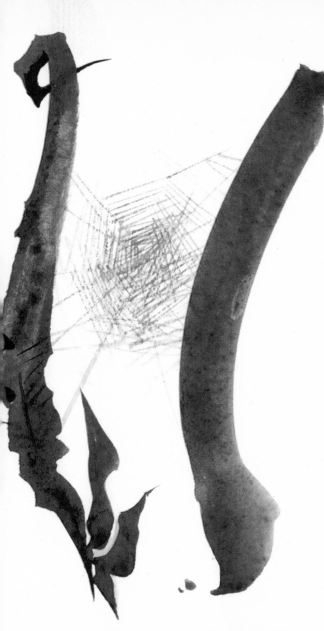

"You may be King of all the beasts, but I'm not afraid of you. You can't do anything more than I can. I'm as good as you any day!"

The Lion flicked his head and twitched his tail angrily when he heard the Gnat's words.

"In fact, King Lion, I am actually stronger than you," the Gnat went on. "What's more, I'll prove it. I'm ready for battle if you are."

And the next moment the Gnat attacked the Lion, biting his face all over his hairless muzzle. The lion jerked his head from side to side, trying to rid himself of the tormenting insect. He growled and roared, and tore at his face with his claws – but it was no use. He could not get rid of the Gnat.

"Oh, go away and leave me in peace!" he cried at last in desperation. "I am no match for an irritating little creature like you!"

"Then you admit you are defeated?" whined the Gnat, hovering around the Lion's nostrils.

"Yes, yes, if you like," answered the Lion testily. "Only GO AWAY!"

Triumphantly humming his triumph, the Gnat flew off.

"I have defeated the mighty Lion! I am stronger than the King of all the beasts!" he exulted.

But in his pride, the Gnat did not see a Spider's web stretched right across the path of his flight. He flew straight into it, and no matter how he struggled, he could not disentangle himself from its silken strands. The fat black Spider who had spun the web crept forward to devour his prey.

"Alas! Oh, cruel fate! To think that I who could defeat the Lion should be destroyed by a mere Spider!" whined the Gnat with his last breath.

THE BOASTFUL GNAT

There was once a Gnat who held a very good opinion of himself for such a tiny insect. All the other creatures grew heartily tired of his boasting, and used to sigh and groan when they heard the whining sound that heralded his coming.

Believe it or not, one day that Gnat had the audacity to approach the great tawny Lion as he lay basking in the heat of the noonday sun.

"Ho, Lion!" called the Gnat as he whined around the Lion's massive head.

THE MOUSE'S BRIDEGROOM

A family of mice once lived in a farmhouse: father, mother, and daughter. The two fond parents thought their daughter was the most beautiful mouse in the world, with her smooth brown coat, her long pink tail, and her delicate whiskers. Another mouse, a bachelor, lived in the barn in the farmyard. He was young and handsome, and he wanted to marry the beautiful Miss Mouse. But her parents did not consider him good enough for their daughter. They wanted her to marry the most powerful being on earth. So they told young Mister Mouse to go away. What did Miss Mouse herself feel about this? She was very sad, for she had fallen in love with the young

mouse from the barn. Her brown coat lost its shine, and her delicate whiskers drooped.

Her parents, however, took no notice. Instead, they set out to find a bridegroom worthy of their daughter.

"Surely the Sun is the most powerful being of all," said Father Mouse. "He shines down upon the earth and ripens the corn in the fields. Let us ask the Sun to marry our daughter."

So the two parent mice stood in the cornfield and asked the bright yellow Sun if he would marry their daughter. They were delighted when the Sun readily agreed to their proposal.

But no sooner had he said "Yes" than Mother Mouse felt a qualm of doubt. "Ask him if he is really the most powerful being of all," she urged Father Mouse.

So Father Mouse asked the Sun: "Are you really the most powerful being of all?"

"No," answered the Sun. "The Rain is more powerful than me. For when a Rain Cloud covers the sky, I am blotted out completely."

Even as he spoke, a great black Rain Cloud drifted across the Sun's face, hiding him from sight.

"In that case, I am very sorry, but you cannot marry our daughter after all!" called Father Mouse, just before he disappeared from view.

Then he addressed the Rain Cloud. "Tell

me, Rain Cloud, are you in fact the most powerful being of all?"

The Rain Cloud scowled down at the two mice in the cornfield. "No, I am not," he replied. "The Wind is more powerful than me. For when the Wind blows, I am torn to shreds and scattered across the sky."

"In that case, I am afraid you may not marry our daughter, either," said Father Mouse.

At that moment, the Wind began to blow. He swept across the sky, scattering the great black Rain Cloud in pieces.

"Oh, Wind!" shouted Father Mouse. "Is it true that you are the most powerful being of all?"

"No, not I!" blustered the Wind. "Do you see that big gray Stone in the corner of the field? It is more powerful than me. I cannot move it, however hard I blow."

"In that case, I am afraid you may not marry our daughter, either" said Father Mouse.

Now the two mice went over to the big gray Stone that stood in one corner of the field. It looked very powerful indeed.

"Are *you* the most powerful being of all?" Father Mouse asked the Stone.

"No, indeed," answered the Stone. "The red Bull is more powerful than me. Every day he comes to sharpen his horns against my surface, breaking off splinters of rock as he does so."

"In that case, I am afraid you may not marry our daughter, either," said Father Mouse.

Next the two mice went to interview the red Bull, who stood tethered in his stall in the barn.

"I think," said Father Mouse, "that you must be the most powerful being of all, and I have come to offer you my daughter."

"You are wrong!" roared the Bull. "This Rope that tethers me is more powerful than I am."

"Oh," said Father Mouse. "In that case, I am afraid you may not marry our daughter, after all."

Now Mother Mouse spoke to the strong Rope that tethered the Bull.

"So you are the most powerful being of all!" she squeaked. "Will you marry our daughter?"

"Much as I would like to marry your daughter," replied the Rope, "I must admit that there is one being even more powerful than me, and that is the young Mouse who lives in this barn. Every night as the Bull stands tethered in his stall, this Mouse comes to gnaw at me with his sharp teeth. In time he will gnaw right through me, and I will break."

"Well!" said Father Mouse. And "Well, well!" exclaimed Mother Mouse. They looked at each other shamefacedly. Then they sought out the handsome young bachelor Mouse who lived in the barn, and begged him to marry their daughter.

Young Mister Mouse was very surprised, and quite overjoyed. As for Miss Mouse, when she heard the good news that she was to marry the bridegroom of her own choice, after all, her coat at once regained its shine, and she preened her delicate whiskers prettily. So the two mice were married, and lived happily ever after.

THE FOX, THE WOLF, AND THE BEAR

In a distant country in the north lived Mekko the Fox, Pekka the Wolf, and Osmo the Bear. One day of sunshine, Mekko suggested to Pekka that they should go into partnership together. Pekka agreed to this.

"The first thing we should do is to make a clearing in the forest and then plant some barley," said Mekko.

So off they went into the dark pine forest, and set about felling trees. This was hard work, and Mekko soon decided he had had enough of it. When Pekka began to gather the brushwood into a pile to burn it, Mekko slipped away and lay down out of sight.

"Heigh-ho, how tired I am!" he yawned. "Why should I do any more work? Let that stupid Pekka do it all!"

"Mekko! Mekko!" called the Wolf. "Aren't you going to help me burn the brushwood?"

"You set it alight," the Fox called back, "I will stay on guard here to see that no flying sparks escape. We don't want to set the whole forest on fire!"

Pekka obediently did as he was told, and that rascal Mekko took a pleasant nap. When all the wood had been burned Pekka said:

"Now we must plant the barley seed in the rich wood ashes. Come and help me, Mekko."

But Mekko replied: "You do the planting, Pekka. I will stay here and scare away the birds, otherwise they will swoop down and peck up every seed!"

"Very well, Mekko," Pekka agreed meekly; and he planted the clearing with barley seed.

Mekko, of course, had no intention of scaring away the birds. All he did was to lie down and go to sleep again.

The year went by, and now it was harvest time. The field of barley that the Wolf had cleared and planted was ready to yield its golden crop. Mekko helped Pekka to cut the grain, and they carried the sheaves into the barn, where they spread them out to dry.

"I have an idea," said Pekka. "Let us ask Osmo the Bear to come and help us with the threshing. Many hands make light work."

"Agreed," said Mekko.

They found the black Bear in the heart of the forest, and put their request to him.

"Certainly I will help you," Osmo said.

When the sheaves of barley were dry, the three friends met to begin the threshing.

"Now we must decide how we shall divide the work," said Pekka.

At once Mekko climbed up into the rafters of the barn. "I will stay up here and support the beams and rafters," he called down. "Otherwise they might fall down on top of you. You'll be all right so long as I stay up here!"

The other two were grateful to the Fox for thinking of their safety. Osmo set to work with the flail, and Pekka winnowed the chaff from the grain. From time to time, Mekko dropped a piece of wood down on top of them.

"You don't know what a difficult time I am having up here, holding up all these rafters!" he told them. "It's a good thing I'm strong, I can tell you!"

Well, the Wolf and the Bear went on working all day long, while the lazy Fox took his ease in the roof. At last the work was finished, and on the floor of the barn lay a heap of straw, a pile of chaff, and a little mound of clean, golden grain.

Then Mekko jumped down from the roof. "I'm glad that's over!" he announced. "I couldn't have held up those rafters much longer!"

"How shall we divide the barley between us?" asked Pekka.

"That's easy," Mekko replied. "There are three of us, and the harvest is already divided into three parts. The biggest heap should naturally go to Osmo the Bear because he is the largest of us. The middle-sized heap should go to you, Pekka. I am the smallest, so the small heap is mine."

The foolish Bear and the stupid Wolf

agreed to this. Osmo took the heap of straw, and Pekka the pile of chaff. But Mekko carried off the little mound of clean, golden grain. Off they went together to grind their meal at the mill. As the millstone turned on Mekko's grain, it made a rough, rasping noise.

"That's strange," Osmo said. "Your grain sounds different than mine and Pekka's, Mekko."

"Mix some sand with yours," Mekko told him. "Then it will sound the same."

So Osmo and Pekka mixed sand with their straw and chaff, and sure enough, they heard a rough, rasping noise when they began to turn their millstones again. Satisfied, they went home believing that they had just as good a store of barley for the long, cold winter as Mekko himself.

On the first day of winter, each of the three friends decided to make some hot, nourishing porridge out of the meal they had ground. Osmo mixed his straw and sand, and stirred it over the fire. But all he got was a black mess that tasted awful.

"Ugh!" he said to himself. "There's something wrong here." And he ambled over to Mekko's den to ask his advice.

He found Mekko stirring a pot of smooth white porridge that tasted very good indeed.

"What is the matter with my porridge?" Osmo asked him. "Yours is white and smooth, but mine is black and awful."

"Did you wash your meal before you put it into the pot?" asked Mekko.

Osmo shook his shaggy head. "Should I have done that?" he asked.

"Certainly," said Mekko. "Take your meal to the river and drop it in the water. As soon as it's clean, take it out again."

Osmo went off, thanking Mekko for his advice. He gathered up all his straw and took it to the river. Then he dropped it in the water. What happened? Why, every straw spread out far and wide, and was carried swiftly away by the current. So that was the end of Osmo's share of the harvest. He ambled home feeling sorry for himself. And there was little for him to eat that winter.

Pekka the Wolf mixed his chaff and

sand and stirred it over the fire. But all he got was a gray mixture that tasted very nasty indeed. So he, too, came to Mekko for advice.

"What is the matter with my porridge?" he asked the Fox. "I see yours is white and smooth. Mine is gray and nasty. Please show me how to make it properly."

"With pleasure," Mekko replied. "Hang your pot beside mine on this chain. Now, before I began to stir mine, I climbed on to the chain and hung over the pot. The heat of the fire melted the fat in my tail and it dripped into the pot. The fat is what makes my porridge so white."

"So that's it!" Pekka cried. Immediately he climbed up and hung onto the chain above his cooking pot. But he did not stay there long. The fire scorched him so badly that he soon jumped down again, howling with pain. When he had recovered, he tried his porridge once more, to see if it tasted any better. But it didn't. It was just as nasty as before.

"I can't tell any difference in it," he complained. Then he said: "Let me try yours, Mekko, to see what it tastes like."

Unknown to Pekka, the artful Mekko had dipped his ladle in Pekka's porridge and dropped some of it into his own pot. Now he said: "Help yourself, by all means. Take some from that spot there; it looks specially good." And he pointed to the place where he had dropped Pekka's own porridge.

So the poor Wolf sampled his own nasty mixture once again, thinking it was Mekko's porridge.

"That's strange," he told Mekko. "I don't like the taste of your porridge either. Do you know, I believe the whole trouble lies in the fact that I just don't like porridge!"

He went off sadly, shaking his head, and a lean time of it he had that winter.

But as for Mekko the Fox, he grinned to himself as he supped his smooth white barley porridge. "I wonder why Pekka doesn't like porridge," he said to himself. "It tastes good to me!"

THE FOX AND THE GINGERBREAD MAN

The Gingerbread Man had been baked brown and crispy. The farmer's wife had given him two currants for eyes, and now she had put him aside to cool.

"My little son shall eat you by and by," she told him.

The Gingerbread Man did not like the sound of that at all. He did not want to be eaten by anyone! "I will go out into the world to seek my fortune," he decided; and as soon as the farmer's wife turned her back, he hopped off the kitchen table and ran out of the door.

How wide was the world! Beyond the farmhouse lay a green hill that sloped down to a broad river. The Gingerbread Man ran helter-skelter down the hill on his thin crispy legs, but when he got to the bottom and saw the river, he did not know what to do.

"How shall I ever get across?" he thought.

At that moment who should come by but the crafty Fox, with his pointed nose and red bushy tail. The Fox licked his lips when he saw the Gingerbread Man, and sniffed his spicy smell.

"Good day, Master Gingerbread! Am I right in thinking that you would like to get across this river?"

"Good day, Sir Fox," the Gingerbread Man replied nervously, eyeing the Fox's sharp white teeth. "I would indeed like to get to the other side of the river."

"Then I will take you," said the Fox. "For I'm going that way myself."

"I – er – I don't think I can accept your offer, Sir Fox," said the Gingerbread Man. "I have an idea you want to eat me!"

The Fox pretended to be hurt by these words. "Eat you! What could have given you such a strange idea? I have no intention of eating you! However, please yourself. If you do want to get across the river, hop onto the tip of my tail while I swim to the other side."

Well, the Gingerbread Man thought he would surely be safe enough if he were that distance away from those sharp white teeth – so he hopped on to the Fox's red bushy tail.

The Fox stepped into the water. When they were a quarter of the way across, the water got deeper.

"You had better come onto my back, Gingerbread Man, for you are getting wet," said the Fox.

The Gingerbread Man was indeed getting wet; his legs were beginning to feel quite soggy. So he moved onto the Fox's back.

When they were halfway across, the water got deeper still.

"You had better come and perch between my ears, Gingerbread Man, for you are getting wet," said the Fox.

And the Gingerbread Man moved up

and perched between the Fox's ears.

When they were three-quarters of the way across, the water was at its deepest, and was beginning to lap up over the fox's head. The Fox said:

"You had better come onto my nose, Gingerbread Man, for you are getting wet." The Gingerbread Man was indeed beginning to feel soggy.

So the Gingerbread Man hopped onto the tip of the Fox's long, pointed nose. What a foolish step that was! He had no sooner settled there than the Fox threw back his head and snapped him all up, every spicy crumb! "My, how good he tasted," thought the fox. And that is how the Gingerbread Man went out into the world and found his fortune.

THE TORTOISE AND
THE HARE

The long-legged Hare skipped over the hillside. In his path lay a large, smooth brown stone. Suddenly a head and four legs emerged from under the stone, and it began to move along the ground. It was not a stone after all. It was a Tortoise in his shell.

The Hare gaped at the Tortoise in amazement.

"What a curious creature you are!" he cried rudely. "And how slowly you creep along the ground! I wonder that you bother to move at all – it must take you such a long time to get anywhere."

The Tortoise peered up at the Hare as he sat grinning at him with his long front teeth.

"Each creature moves at its own pace," he said wisely. "I creep along slowly but surely. Who knows? It may be that I reach my destination more quickly than a fleet-footed animal like you."

"What nonsense!" retorted the Hare. "I've never heard of anything so absurd! How could you possibly reach your destination more quickly than me? I can run as fast as the wind. You crawl along so slowly that it's difficult to tell whether you are moving or not."

The Tortoise sighed. "There is only one way of settling our dispute. We must run a race against each other."

How the Hare laughed. "All right," he agreed, "let us run a race. The course shall be from this hilltop to the tall oak tree that grows in the valley. Are you ready? Are you steady? *Go!*"

And with a bound the Hare leaped from the hilltop and left the Tortoise far behind him. After he had run a little distance, he thought to himself: "There's no need to hurry! I could win this race at walking-pace. It will be ages before that slowpoke of a Tortoise comes in sight again." He yawned. "The sun is hot. I feel sleepy. I think I will take a little nap. There will be plenty of time to win the race when I wake up."

And the Hare lay down beside a clump of grass and was soon fast asleep.

Meanwhile, way back on the hillside, the Tortoise crept slowly along, never pausing or stopping in his progress. Inch by inch he covered the ground.

The day wore on. The sun moved westward. Still the Hare slept soundly, and still the Tortoise plodded on. Eventually the Tortoise passed by the clump of grass where the Hare lay sleeping, but the Hare did not hear him go by.

It was late when the Hare woke up at last. He glanced back, trying to see the Tortoise through the dusk.

"He's even slower than I thought," he told himself. "Oh, well, I suppose I may as well go on to the oak tree, though I expect it will be midnight before he shows up!"

Imagine the Hare's astonishment when he arrived at the oak tree to find the Tortoise there before him.

"How . . . when . . . why . . . ?" he spluttered helplessly.

The Tortoise looked at the Hare and smiled. "How did I win the race? By plodding steadily along. When did I win it? When I passed you asleep on the hillside. Why did I win? Because I allowed nothing to turn me aside from the course. And now, my fleet-footed friend, you may understand what I meant when I said that maybe I could travel more quickly than you."

THE MOUSE-DEER
AND THE CROCODILE

The Mouse-Deer was one of the smallest animals in the jungle. But he was brave and clever, and the other creatures respected him.

One fine day, Mouse-Deer came down to the wide, oozy river, where the Hippopotamus wallowed in the mud and old man Crocodile floated in the water. Mouse-Deer wanted to reach the other side of the river, but there was no way to get across. Then he had an idea.

"Ho, old man Crocodile!" he called. "I am very sorry for you!"

Old Man Crocodile thrashed his tail. "Why do you feel sorry for me, little Mouse-Deer?" he asked.

"I feel sorry for you because you have so few relatives. I have lots of brothers and sisters, plenty of uncles and aunts, and dozens of cousins! But you have no relatives at all, you poor thing."

"You do not know what you are talking about, you foolish little creature," the Crocodile replied, "Why, I have scores of relatives! I am sure there are more mem-

bers of my family than there are of yours."

Mouse-Deer smiled. "I doubt it," he said. "Why, there are so many of us that whenever we hold a family reunion you cannot see a blade of grass for miles around!"

"That's nothing," retorted old man Crocodile. "There are so many of us that whenever *we* hold a family reunion, the first-comer has to make his voice carry for miles so that the last-comer can hear what he is saying."

The argument grew more and more heated, and at last the Mouse-Deer said: "There is only one way of settling our dispute. You must call all the members of your family together, and I will count them carefully."

"Very well," the Crocodile agreed, "I will go at once to summon all my relatives."

He swam away, and the Mouse-Deer waited on the bank of the wide, oozy river. It was not long before he saw old man Crocodile returning – and with him were scores and scores of other crocodiles: his wife, his children, his grandchildren, his sisters, brothers, cousins . . .

The Mouse-Deer calmly surveyed this great crowd of crocodiles. Then he said to old man Crocodile: "It would be easiest for me to count your relatives if they were to arrange themselves in a long line, stretching from this side of the river to the other."

"Very well," said old man Crocodile; and he ordered his relatives to arrange themselves in just that way.

As soon as this was done, the little Mouse-Deer leaped down onto the back of the first Crocodile.

"One-two-three-four-five-six-seven!" he cried, skipping nimbly along the whole bridge of Crocodiles, until he had reached the other side of the river.

When he had jumped safely ashore on to the farther bank, he turned and laughed at all the Crocodiles.

"You silly creatures!" he mocked them. "I don't care how many of you there are. What does it matter to me? All I wanted was a way to cross the river. Thank you for providing it! Farewell, old man Crocodile!"

You can imagine how surprised and how angry old man Crocodile was when he realized the Mouse-Deer had tricked him! He thrashed the water with his tail and bellowed threats that he would get even with the Mouse-Deer one day.

But I doubt if the Mouse-Deer heard him, for by that time he had scampered away into the heart of his jungle home.

THE CHICKEN, THE CAT AND THE CAKE

A red Hen and her little yellow Chicken lived together in the farmyard. One day the Chicken said to his mother: "Please, will you make me a cake?"

"Yes, I will make you a cake," replied the red Hen, "but first you must fetch me some firewood, so that I may light a fire to bake the cake."

The little yellow Chicken ran into the farmhouse kitchen. Stacked beside the hearth was a heap of kindling, and he helped himself. But alas! He did not see the big black Cat, who was lying behind the stack of wood. The cat pounced upon the little yellow Chicken.

"Let me go! Let me go!" he cheeped. "My mother is baking a cake, and if you let me go free, you shall have a piece of it to eat."

The big black Cat was very fond of cake. "Very well," she agreed, "I will let you go, on condition that you bring me a slice of cake."

Then the little yellow Chicken ran back to his mother with his bundle of wood.

"Oh mother, oh mother!" he cried. "The big black Cat caught hold of me, and only let me go free on condition that I would give her a slice of cake to eat."

"Don't worry, little Chicken," said the red Hen, "I will bake such a large cake that there will be plenty for you and the big black Cat."

She lit the fire and baked a big, big cake. How good it smelled! How the little yellow Chicken longed to eat it up! As soon as it was cool, his mother said: "Now you may eat your cake. But be sure to leave a piece for the big black Cat."

The little yellow Chicken carried the cake into a corner of the henhouse. He took one mouthful. How delicious it was! He took another mouthful . . . then another . . . and another. And what do you think? That greedy little Chicken quite forgot about leaving a piece for the big black Cat.

"Oh mother, oh mother, what shall I do?" he cheeped. "I have eaten up all the cake, every crumb!"

"You naughty little Chicken!" scolded the red Hen.

At that moment, the big black Cat came slinking round the side of the henhouse. She had sniffed the tasty smell of the cake, and had come to claim her share of it.

"Quick, follow me, little Chicken!" the red Hen cackled. She ran as fast as she could toward the farmhouse, and the little yellow Chicken ran beside her. They went into the kitchen, and the red Hen looked around for a place to hide. She saw a big stone jar, and hopped inside it; and the little yellow Chicken hopped in after her.

When the big black Cat saw the red Hen and her little yellow Chicken running away, she was very angry indeed. "Where is my piece of cake?" she called. "Is this the way you repay my kindness in letting you go free, you greedy little Chicken? You had better look out, for now I am coming to eat you up – and the red Hen, too!"

The Cat came into the farmhouse, and looked around the kitchen. But she could not see the red Hen and her little yellow Chicken anywhere.

Inside the big stone jar, the Hen and the Chicken shivered with fright as they heard the big black Cat padding about the room.

Suddenly the little Chicken whispered: "Oh, mother, oh, mother, I want to sneeze!"

"Don't sneeze, little Chicken, whatever you do!" replied his mother. "The Cat will hear you, and then she will find us, and that will be the end of *that*!'

A few moments went by, and then the little Chicken said again: "Oh mother, oh mother, I want to sneeze *very much*!'

"You must not sneeze, little Chicken," his mother answered.

They waited inside the jar, and presently the Cat stopped prowling around the kitchen. She sat down in the doorway.

"I am sure the red Hen and the little yellow Chicken have hidden themselves somewhere in this kitchen," she thought to herself. "If I wait and watch, sooner or later they will come out. Then I will pounce on them and eat them up!"

And now, for the third time, the little yellow Chicken said to the red Hen: "Oh mother, oh mother, I want to sneeze *very much indeed*!"

The red Hen listened carefully, but she could no longer hear the big black Cat prowling around outside.

"Very well, little Chicken," she said. "You may sneeze a tiny sneeze."

So the little yellow Chicken opened his beak and sneezed. He meant to sneeze a tiny sneeze, but instead he sneezed an enormous sneeze. *Atishoo! Atishoo! Atishoo!*

It was such a loud sneeze that the big stone jar broke in pieces, and so the red Hen and her Chicken lost their hiding-place. Happily for them, however, the big black Cat was so frightened by the sudden *crash* that she all but leaped out of her skin! She ran away as fast as she could, and never came near the farmyard again, and so the red Hen and her little yellow Chicken returned to the henhouse none the worse for their adventure.

THE CROW AND THE WREN

The Crow is a large, black bird with a curved beak and beady eyes. His voice is harsh and he is cruel. The Wren is a tiny brown bird. She cheeps a little song, and has a timid nature. One day the Crow seized the Wren in his claws.

"I am going to eat you, little Wren!" he said.

"Oh, my dear little fledgling, who will look after you when I am gone!" cried the Wren pitifully.

When the Crow heard this, he paused. "The Wren must be old and tough," he thought. "But her fledgling will be young and tender." So he said to the Wren: "I will let you go on condition that you bring your little fledgling to me on the seventh day from now."

"I promise! I promise!" cheeped the Wren.

And the Crow let her go.

On the seventh day, he came to the Wren's nest and demanded her fledgling.

"Before you eat my fledgling, you must clean your dirty beak," the Wren told him. "Let me see you wash it in some water."

"Very well," said the Crow, "I will go and fetch some water."

He spread his wings and flew away. Soon he came to a stream, and called out in his harsh voice:

"Water, water, come with me
To wash my beak
To eat the little Wren!"

"How can I come with you unless you bring a pot to carry me in?" gurgled the water.

So the Crow spread his wings again and flew away to find a pot. Presently he saw one lying in the grass, and swooped to pick it up.

"Pot, pot, come with me
To hold the water
To wash my beak
To eat the little Wren!" he called.

"I would come with you," replied the Pot, "but there is a hole in my side, and the water would leak out. You will have to get some mud to mend the hole."

The Crow flew off once more, and alighted beside a pool of mud.

"Mud, mud, come with me
To mend the Pot
To hold the water
To wash my beak
To eat the little Wren!"

"I would come with you," answered the Mud, "but the hot sun has made me hard and dry. You must ask the Buffalo to come and wallow here."

So the Crow flew off to look for the Buffalo. Not far away he found him lying on the ground. The Crow hopped up to him and said:

"Buffalo, buffalo, come with me
To wallow in the mud
To mend the pot
To hold the water
To wash my beak
To eat the little Wren!"

"I would come with you," said the Buffalo, "but I am weak from hunger. I have not the strength to walk to the pool of mud. Go and get me some grass to eat. Then I will come."

The Crow left the Buffalo and flew to a clump of grass.

"Grass, grass, come with me
To feed the Buffalo
To wallow in the mud

To mend the pot
To hold the water
To wash my beak
To eat the little Wren!''

''I would come with you,'' said the Grass, ''but the Buffalo is such a large animal that he needs a great deal to eat, more than I can provide at the moment. However, if you can find me more land, I will spread out until there is enough of me to satisfy the Buffalo.''

The Crow flew away yet again, and circled above a forest of trees.

''Land, land, come with me
To grow the grass
To feed the Buffalo
To wallow in the mud
To mend the pot
To hold the water
To wash my beak
To eat the little Wren!''

''I would come with you,'' answered the Land, ''but as you can see, I am covered with trees. The grass cannot grow on me until the trees have gone.''

So the Crow called to the trees:

''Trees, trees, go away
To clear the land
To grow the grass
To feed the Buffalo
To wallow in the mud
To mend the pot
To hold the water
To wash my beak
To eat the little Wren!''

''We would go away,'' the Trees replied, rustling their branches, ''but we cannot move. Our roots are held firmly in the earth. Only fire could move us from the land.''

Once more the Crow spread his wings and flew away. In a village he found a fire.

''Fire, fire, come with me
To move the trees
To clear the land
To grow the grass
To feed the Buffalo
To wallow in the mud
To mend the pot

To hold the water
To wash my beak
To eat the little Wren!''

''Yes, I will come with you!'' cracked the Fire, and it leaped up to meet him. ''At last!'' thought the wicked Crow. ''Now I will be able to eat that juicy little Wren for my dinner after all!'' But alas! The orange and yellow flames were so fierce that they burned the Crow until there was nothing left of him. And so – the trees did not move, the land was not cleared, the grass did not grow, the Buffalo stayed hungry, the mud remained hard, the hole in the pot was not mended, the water stayed where it was, and the Crow did not eat the little Wren after all.

MONKEY IS KING

One fine day long ago the animals gathered together in a forest clearing to decide which of them should be elected king. Every animal was there, from the largest and strongest to the smallest and weakest. The massive Elephant, with his curved tusks and loose gray skin, stood at the edge of the clearing, beside a pool of water. The elegant Giraffe, with his spotted hide, reached up to the lowest branches of the trees and ate the sweet green leaves. The tawny maned Lion stalked proudly into the assembly; and the timid Deer and the wild Goat kept their distance from him. The cunning-eyed Wolf lurked in the shade, the Snake slithered from its hole, the Rabbits crept from their burrows, and

the shaggy Bear lumbered in from the forest where he had been stealing honey from the wild bees. They followed him in a swarm, buzzing angrily over the loss of their golden treasure. In the trees, the Birds chattered and called to each other. Even the humble Beetle, glossy and black, was there to see what would happen.

One by one the animals showed what they could do. The Elephant dipped his trunk into the pool, and sprayed water all over everyone around him. The Birds croaked and sang. The Fox asked clever riddles. The Lion opened his mouth and made the clearing echo with his mighty roar – whereupon the Deer kicked up her

heels and ran as fast as the wind.

The other animals applauded each performer in turn. They were especially impressed by the Fox's cleverness. The Fox grinned to himself, showing his sharp teeth. He was sure he would be chosen as king.

Then it was the Monkey's turn. The Monkey was agile and nimble-footed..His movements were quick and skillful. He could swing from branch to branch across the treetops. And now he danced before all the other animals. How Monkey danced! He leaped and turned and pranced and skipped. And in his dance he mimicked the other animals around him, imitating the clumsy Bear, the nervous Rabbits with their twitching noses, the sinuous Snake, the graceful Giraffe . . .

How the watchers in the forest clearing enjoyed Monkey's dance! This was even better than the Fox's riddles. Now they were sure they wanted the Monkey to be their king.

"The Monkey must be king! We choose the monkey!" they shouted.

The Monkey strutted with pride, throwing out his chest; but the Fox was filled with jealousy. He decided to prove how stupid the other animals had been to choose Monkey as their king. He did not show his jealousy, for that is not the way of foxes. He smiled at the Monkey and invited him to walk through the forest. Presently they came to a place where a snare lay half-hidden in the grass. The snare was baited with a juicy piece of meat.

"See, King Monkey, here is a choice tidbit that I have kept for you," the Fox said, pointing to the meat. "I would be honored if you would take it and eat it."

The Monkey licked his lips. He spent most of his time among the treetops. There were no snares in the treetops. Unsuspectingly, he went to take the meat. *Snap*! He was caught fast in the snare, unable to move. Furiously he twisted his head round to look at the Fox, who stood smiling with pleasure at the success of his crafty plan to make the Monkey look stupid.

"How dare you make me walk into this trap!" the Monkey gibbered. "I am king of all the animals! How dare you play such a trick on me!"

The Fox burst out laughing. "You, the king of the animals!" he jeered. "Fancy a fool like you being elected king! Why, even the youngest Rabbit would not be so stupid as to walk into a snare the way you did! You the king? Pah! An Ant would make a better one!"

And waving his bushy tail in the air, the Fox walked slowly away from the helpless Monkey.

THE TRAVELING MUSICIANS

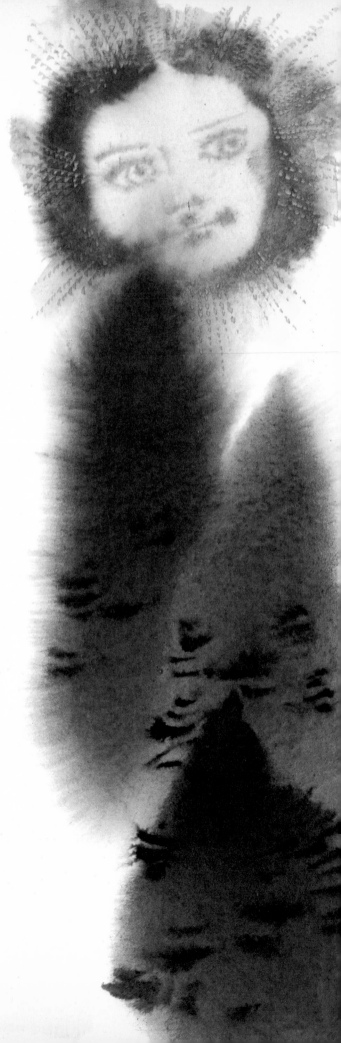

There was once a long-eared Ass who had served his master faithfully for many years. But now he was growing old and could no longer work as hard as he used to. One day, as he grazed in a field of thistles, he heard his master say: "It is time to put an end to this old Ass." The Ass did not like the sound of that at all; so he kicked up his heels, jumped over the hedge, and ran away as fast as he could. Soon he was trotting down the high road that led toward the town.

"I will go to town and try my luck as a musician," he thought to himself. "I have a fine musical voice." And he brayed loud and clear.

A little farther along the road he came upon an old brown Dog panting by the wayside.

"What ails you, friend?" the Ass inquired. "Why are you so out of breath?"

"Alas," said the Dog, "I am growing old, and can no longer hunt with my master. He wanted to put an end to me — so I have run away."

"In that case," said the Ass, "we are companions in misfortune. I am going to town to try my luck as a musician. Come with me."

"Very well," the Dog agreed. "I have a fine musical voice." And he barked loudly.

They went on their way, and before long they met a sleek black Cat sitting in the middle of the road, with a face as dismal as three rainy days.

"What is the matter with you?" asked the Ass. "Why do you look so miserable?"

"Alas!" said the Cat. "I am growing old, and cannot chase after the mice as I used to. My mistress was going to drown me in the well, so I have run away."

"In that case," said the Ass, "we are all three companions in misfortune. The Dog and I are going to town to try our luck as musicians. Will you join us?"

112

"Very well," the Cat agreed. "I have a fine musical voice," And she mewed shrilly in a very pleasant tone.

They journeyed on together, and presently they passed by a farmyard. A Cock with a bright red comb was perched on the gatepost, crowing for all he was worth.

"That's a good song, old rooster!" the Ass greeted him. "But why do you make so much noise?"

"Alas," said the Cock, "this morning I woke the farmer's wife and crowed out that it was fine weather for washing day – but she did not thank me for my trouble. She is going to make broth out of me for tomorrow's dinner: so I am crowing as hard as I can while there is breath left in me."

"What a dreadful fate!" said the Ass. "Why don't you join my friends and me instead? We are going to town to try our luck as musicians. I am sure your splendid voice will be much admired by all the townspeople there."

"Very well," agreed the Cock, "I will come with you."

So all the four companions traveled the

road to town together: the long-eared Ass, the brown Dog, the sleek black Cat, and the Cock with his bright red comb.

But it was a long way to the town, and when dusk fell they decided to spend the night in a wood. The Ass and the Dog lay down under a tall tree, and the Cat found a resting place in the branches. The Cock, however, flew right to the top of the tree, and before he settled down to sleep, he looked all around him. Away in the distance he spied something shining. So he called down to his companions: "There must be a house nearby, for I can see a light."

"Well, then," said the Ass, "let us see if we can find shelter there – for this tree does not provide very good lodging."

They went through the wood in the direction of the light, and at last they came to a house. The Ass went up to the window and peered inside.

"What do you see, Long Ears?" asked the Cock.

"I see a table covered with good things to eat and drink," the Ass replied. "And sitting around the table I see a band of robbers making merry."

"How I wish we could enjoy those good things to eat and drink!" said the Cock.

"If only we could get into the house!" sighed the Ass.

Then all four animals put their heads together and made a bold plan to drive the robbers away. First, the Ass stood upright, planting his forefeet on the window sill. Next, the Dog scrambled on to his back. Then the Cat leaped up to the Dog's shoulders. Finally, the Cock flew up and sat on the Cat's head. The Ass gave a signal, and they began to make music all together. The Ass brayed, the Dog barked, the Cat mewed, and the Cock crowed. What a terrible din it was! Then they all burst through the window, shattering the glass.

The robbers sprang up from the table, trembling with fear, and fled into the wood.

And now the four traveling musicians sat down to eat and drink all the good things on the table. When they were satisfied, they put out the lamp and settled down to sleep. The Ass lay down on a heap of straw in the yard. The Dog stretched himself out behind the door. The Cat curled up beside the kitchen hearth. The Cock flew up into the rafters. Soon they were all asleep.

Meanwhile, out in the wood, the robbers had got over their first alarm. "We should not have allowed ourselves to be frightened out of our wits," said the robber chief. "It seems quiet enough now." And he ordered one of the other robbers to return to the house to find out what had happened.

This robber came to the dark house. Nothing stirred, so he went into the kitchen and took out a match, intending to light the lamp. He saw the Cat's eyes glinting by the hearth, and mistook them for live coals — so he held the match out to them. At once the Cat sprang in his face, spitting and scratching. The robber was terribly frightened and ran to the door, where the Dog jumped up and bit his leg; and as he rushed through the yard, the Ass rose up from his heap of straw and kicked him. Then the Cock, wakened by all the disturbance, cried out from the rafters: "Cock-a-doodle-do!"

The Robber ran back to his cronies. "Oh!" he cried. "There is a horrible old witch in the kitchen who spat at me and scratched me with her long fingernails. Behind the door stands a man with a knife, who stabbed me in the leg. In the yard a black monster rose up and hit me with a club. And from the rafters the devil himself called out: 'Bring the rogue up here to me!'"

When they heard this, the robbers made off as fast as they could, and never went near the house again. But the long-eared Ass, the brown Dog, the sleek black Cat, and the Cock with his bright red comb found the place suited them so well that they gave up the idea of going to town, and decided to stay there. And they are living there still.

THE TIGER,
THE MOUSE-DEER
AND THE DOG

Harimau the ferocious Tiger was hungry.
He prowled through the teakwood forest
looking for something to eat. As soon as
the other jungle creatures caught sight of
his black and orange body moving among
the undergrowth, they ran away to hide.
And so Harimau could not find anything
to satisfy his hunger.

There were plenty of birds, to be sure,
perched in the leafy boughs overhead,
but tigers cannot climb trees. The long
day went by, and Harimau got hungrier
and hungrier.

At last, however, he saw a little Mouse-
Deer stretched out along a fallen tree
trunk, fast asleep.

"Ha!" cried Harimau, "that is just the
sort of juicy tidbit I've been trying to find

all day long!" And he crept forward.

But before he could spring upon the Mouse-Deer and eat him, a long-tailed Scissor Bird sitting in a treetop, who saw the terrible danger that threatened the Mouse-Deer, cried loudly: "Look out! Look out!" And the little Mouse-Deer woke up with a start.

You can imagine what a fright he got when he saw the ferocious Tiger crouching there before him! In a moment he leaped from the tree trunk and bounded away – and Harimau went after him, roaring and bellowing as he did so.

"You shan't escape me!" he roared as the little Mouse-Deer fled through the jungle.

The Mouse-Deer ran as fast as he could,

but he knew that Harimau was gaining on him. He felt the Tiger's hot breath on his back. Now he came to the edge of the jungle. An enormous heap of rocks loomed up in front of him. Mouse-Deer scrabbled desperately up the rocks, and suddenly he fell headlong into a deep ravine. The ravine was too narrow for Harimau to go down after the Mouse-Deer. Roaring with disappointment, he went away.

But now Mouse-Deer found himself in a worse predicament then ever. True, he had escaped the Tiger, but how was he to get out of the ravine? The rocky walls were steep and smooth, and he was such a little animal that he could not jump out. It seemed that he must stay there until he died of starvation.

"I might as well have provided old Harimau's dinner after all!" he told himself sadly.

He thought longingly of the succulent green bamboo shoots that he loved to eat, and groaned and wept at his plight.

It wasn't long, however, before a wild Dog came bounding over the rocks. The Dog paused on the edge of the ravine. He

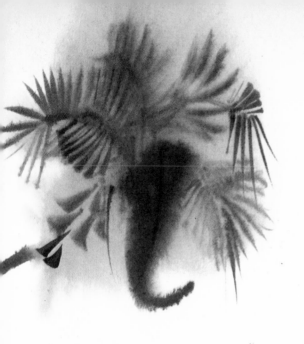

was just about to jump across it when the Mouse-Deer called up to him:

"Hallo, friend Dog! Hallo!"

The dog was most surprised to hear this faint voice from the bottom of the ravine. He peered down.

"Hallo, friend Mouse-Deer! How did you get down there?" he asked.

Now the Mouse-Deer was a clever little creature. As soon as he caught sight of the Dog, he had thought of a plan whereby he might escape from his prison. So now he said:

"I came down here because it was the safest hiding place I could find."

"Why are you hiding?" asked the Dog.

The Mouse-Deer pretended to be astonished. "Haven't you heard the dreadful news?" he asked. "Surely you know that the heavens are about to fall down! That is why I am hiding here. I'm sure I shall be quite safe in this deep, dry ravine."

The Dog was a gullible creature. When he heard the Mouse-Deer's words, he looked very worried. "The heavens are about to fall down!" he repeated. "That is dreadful news indeed!" He gazed down at the Mouse-Deer. "Do you think, friend Mouse-Deer, that there would be room for two of us in that deep, dry ravine of yours?"

"There might be," the Mouse-Deer replied cautiously.

The Dog peered anxiously at the sky. "Please let me come down and join you," he pleaded.

"Very well, friend Dog," said the Mouse-Deer, "you may come down."

And so the foolish Dog jumped down between the rocks and joined the little Mouse-Deer at the bottom of the ravine.

For a while they crouched there together. At last, after several hours had gone by, the Dog said: "It seems to be taking a very long time for the heavens to fall down, my friend."

"I cannot understand it," answered the Mouse-Deer. "I was told that they were about to fall down at any moment. That was hours ago. Perhaps there has been some mistake. I tell you what, my friend – just let me stand on your shoulders, so that I can look out and see what is happening."

The Dog thought this was a very brave suggestion for the Mouse-Deer to make, and he readily agreed to it. "Be careful!" he warned. "We don't want the sky to fall on your head as soon as you put it outside."

The cunning Mouse-Deer smiled to himself.

"I'll be careful, friend Dog, never fear!" he replied.

Then the Dog stood on his hind legs, and the Mouse-Deer scrambled up his back and on to his shoulders. All at once he gave a tremendous leap, and landed safe and sound outside the ravine. He had escaped! He ran back to his home in the teakwood forest to look for some juicy bamboo shoots to eat, and as he ran he laughed and laughed to think how easily he had tricked the wild Dog.

WHY THE RABBIT'S NOSE TWITCHES

The fat green Frog was jealous because all the jungle animals praised the Rabbit for his wisdom. "I will play a trick upon the Rabbit!" he said to himself. He hid beneath a stone, and when he saw the Rabbit coming toward him, he jumped out suddenly and shouted in a very loud voice: "Ong-ing!"

The Rabbit was so startled that he leaped ten feet off the ground, and landed on top of a Pumpkin. The Pumpkin shot out from under the Rabbit, rolled down a slope, and bumped into a Sessamin Plant, scattering its seeds far and wide. A Wild Fowl was flying over the Sessamin Plant, and some of the seeds got in his eyes, so that he could not see. He alighted on a Bamboo Plant. But the Bamboo Plant was not strong enough to bear the weight of the Wild Fowl. It broke, and fell on a Snake that lay curled up on the ground below. The Snake darted away and slithered up into a tree, where a Monkey sat eating a ripe Banana. The Monkey got a terrible fright and dropped the Banana. It fell down *plop* on top of a Tiger's head. The Tiger had been enjoying a quiet snooze. He woke up in a temper and shouted crossly at the Banana.

"How dare you disturb me while I was asleep!"

"Oh sir, please don't be angry with me," said the Banana. "It was not my fault. The Monkey dropped me."

The Tiger roared, and accused the Monkey of waking him up.

"Oh, sir, it had nothing to do with me," cried the Monkey. "The Snake slithered up into my tree."

The Tiger chased the Snake and caught him. "So you are the culprit!" he snarled.

"Oh sir, don't blame it on me," hissed the Snake. "The Bamboo Plant fell on me."

The Tiger went up to the Bamboo Plant. "It was all your fault!" he roared.

120

"Oh sir, I could not help it," replied the Bamboo Plant. "The Wild Fowl alighted on me."

The Tiger sprang upon the Wild Fowl. "Now I know who is to blame!" he cried.

"Oh sir," cackled the Wild Fowl, "the Sessamin Plant threw its seeds into my eyes and I could not see."

The Tiger soon found the Sessamin Plant, "So it was you!" he said. By this time his voice was becoming quite hoarse.

"Oh sir," answered the Sessamin Plant, "it was the Pumpkin that bumped into me."

The Tiger seized hold of the Pumpkin. "What have you got to say for yourself?" he asked.

"Oh sir," said the Pumpkin, "indeed it was the Rabbit who landed on top of me and sent me flying."

So at last the Tiger came to the Rabbit. "Now I know that you are the wretch who dared to disturb my sleep!" he said. "I am going to eat you up."

"Oh sir, please don't do that!" squeaked the Rabbit. "It wasn't really I who woke you up. The fat green Frog jumped out at me from under that stone."

The Tiger sniffed under the stone, but there was no sign of the fat green Frog, for he had fled while the going was good.

"You are a liar," said the Tiger to the Rabbit. "There is no Frog under the stone."

The poor Rabbit stood gazing at the Tiger in terror. He could think of no way out of this predicament. For once his wits had deserted him. He trembled all over, from the tips of his ears to his tail. His whiskers quivered, and his little pink nose twitched and twitched and twitched.

Suddenly the Tiger burst into roars of laughter to see the Rabbit's nose twitching and twitching and twitching. "I will let you go after all!" he said. "Be off before I lose my temper again!"

The Rabbit needed no second bidding; he scampered away as fast as his legs would carry him. And to this day, the Rabbit's nose twitches and twitches and twitches.

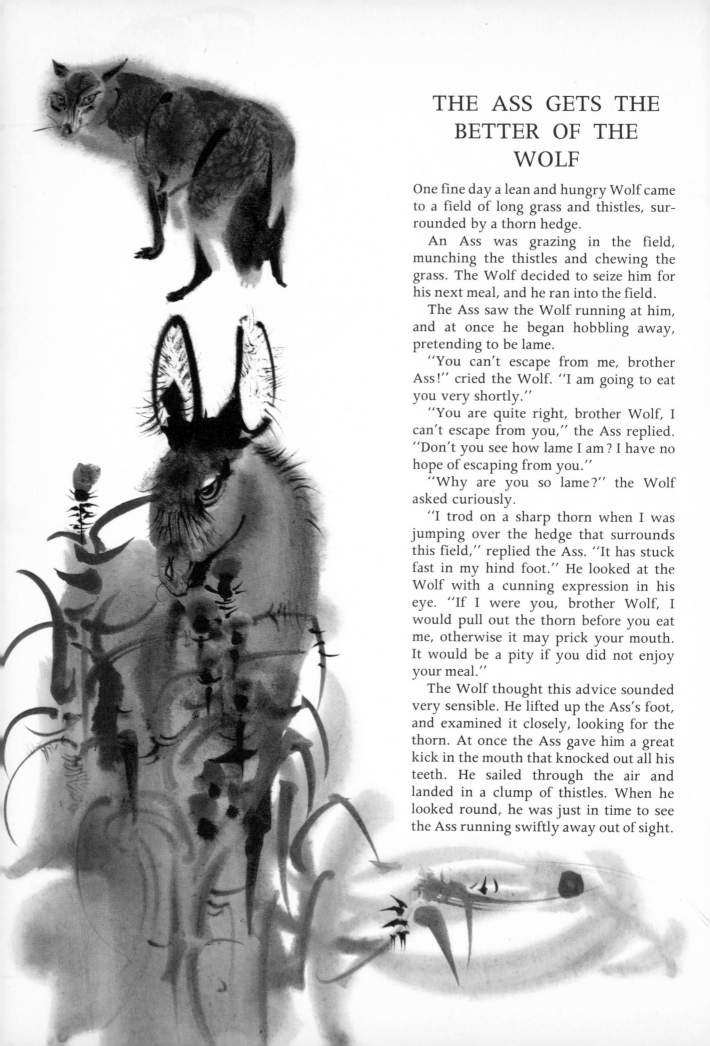

THE ASS GETS THE BETTER OF THE WOLF

One fine day a lean and hungry Wolf came to a field of long grass and thistles, surrounded by a thorn hedge.

An Ass was grazing in the field, munching the thistles and chewing the grass. The Wolf decided to seize him for his next meal, and he ran into the field.

The Ass saw the Wolf running at him, and at once he began hobbling away, pretending to be lame.

"You can't escape from me, brother Ass!" cried the Wolf. "I am going to eat you very shortly."

"You are quite right, brother Wolf, I can't escape from you," the Ass replied. "Don't you see how lame I am? I have no hope of escaping from you."

"Why are you so lame?" the Wolf asked curiously.

"I trod on a sharp thorn when I was jumping over the hedge that surrounds this field," replied the Ass. "It has stuck fast in my hind foot." He looked at the Wolf with a cunning expression in his eye. "If I were you, brother Wolf, I would pull out the thorn before you eat me, otherwise it may prick your mouth. It would be a pity if you did not enjoy your meal."

The Wolf thought this advice sounded very sensible. He lifted up the Ass's foot, and examined it closely, looking for the thorn. At once the Ass gave him a great kick in the mouth that knocked out all his teeth. He sailed through the air and landed in a clump of thistles. When he looked round, he was just in time to see the Ass running swiftly away out of sight.

RAMBÉ AND AMBÉ

In the mysterious, far-off land of Tibet, there was once a Cat who lived in a temple that was overrun with Mice. For many years, the Cat caught as many Mice as she wanted with the greatest of ease, and lived a pleasant and peaceful life. But as time passed, she grew old and stiff, and found she could no longer catch the Mice so easily. She was not quick enough, and they were able to scamper away before she had time to pounce on them.

The Cat, however, was a cunning creature. She said to herself: "If I can no longer obtain my food by skill in hunting, I must use my wits instead."

One day, she called all the Mice to a meeting. The Mice crept cautiously out of their holes, noses twitching and tails quivering, for they did not trust the Cat. But the Cat promised not to harm them, and said:

"I have called you together because I have something important to say to you. I have led a bad, wicked life. Now that I am old, I repent of the annoyance and inconvenience I have caused you in the past. In future, things will be different. I intend to devote myself to religious contemplation, and I will no longer molest you. From now on, you will be able to run about as freely as you like, and need fear no harm from me." She paused. "All I ask," she went on, "is that twice each day you file past me and bow before me in turn, to show your gratitude for my mercy and kindness."

The Mice were overjoyed when they heard this long speech from their former enemy the Cat, and they promised eagerly to do as she asked. Why! It would be worth the humiliation of bowing to the cat if they didn't have to worry about running away from her all the time.

Accordingly, that evening the Cat came

and took her place on a cushion at one end
of the largest room in the temple, and the
Mice, who had spent the day running
about quite freely, came past her one by
one, in single file. And as each Mouse
stood before the Cat, he gave a deep bow.

Now you shall understand the cunning
of the Cat. For as soon as the procession
had all passed by with the exception of
the one last little Mouse, the Cat suddenly
pounced and seized the last Mouse in her
claws, and devoured him. And none of the
others who had gone before noticed.

This went on for some time. Twice each
day the Mice filed past the Cat to show
their gratitude for her mercy and kindness, and twice each day the Cat pounced
upon the last Mouse of all, and ate him up.

"This is a much easier way of getting my
food than hunting for it!" smirked the Cat.

Now among the Mice of the temple were
two brothers called Rambé and Ambé,
who were more intelligent than the rest
of their kind. They soon noticed that the
number of Mice in the temple seemed to
be dwindling considerably, in spite of the
fact that the Cat had promised to molest
them no longer. They suspected the Cat of
foul play, and so they laid a clever plan.
They arranged that in future, Rambé
would always walk in the very front of
the procession of Mice as they paid their
respects to the Cat, and Ambé would
bring up the rear. All the time the procession continued, Rambé would call out
to Ambé, and Ambé would reply. In this
way they would be certain that the same
number of mice remained in the procession.

The next evening, therefore, the Mice
started off with Rambé at their head and
Ambé last of all. As soon as Rambé had
bowed before the Cat on her cushion, he
squeaked loudly:

"Are you still there, brother Ambé?"

And from the rear of the procession,
Ambé squeaked back: "I am still here,
brother Rambé!"

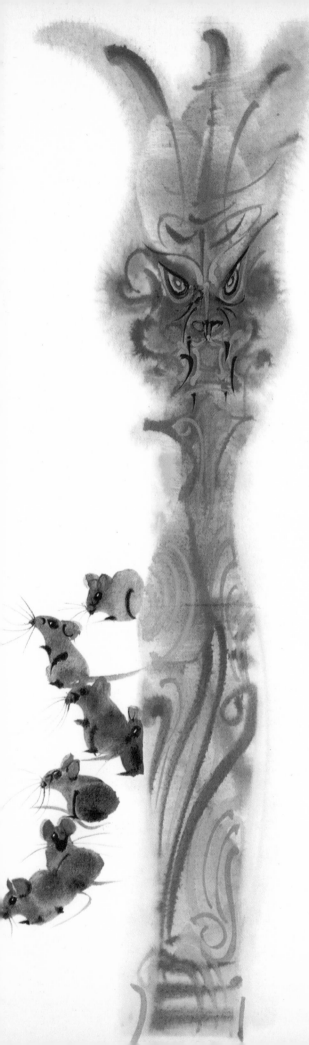

So they continued to call out to each other until Ambé was safely past the Cat — for she did not dare to pounce on him so long as his brother went on calling to him.

The Cat was disappointed that she had missed her supper that night. However, she thought it was only by chance that the two brothers had taken their places at the head and the rear of the procession. Next time the Mice filed past, she hoped to pounce on the last one of all just as she did before. Imagine her dismay when Rambé and Ambé took up the same places in the procession next morning! Rambé called to Ambé, and Ambé called back to Rambé until every Mouse had gone by, and once again the Cat went hungry.

This time the Cat began to suspect that the Mice were deliberately foiling her cunning plan. However, she decided to give them one more trial. That evening, therefore, she took her place on the cushion as usual, and waited for the Mice to appear.

In the meantime, Rambé and Ambé had warned the other Mice to be ready to take flight at once if the Cat showed any anger. Then the procession started out, with Rambé in the lead and Ambé at the rear.

No sooner had Rambé bowed before the Cat than he squeaked loudly: "Are you still there, brother Ambé?"

"I am still here, brother Rambé!" came the shrill squeak from the rear.

This was more than the Cat could stand. She spat with rage and leaped into the midst of the procession. But the Mice, forewarned, scampered off to their holes before she could pounce on any of them. In no time at all there was not a Mouse to be seen.

After this, the Mice put no more trust in the treacherous Cat, but were careful to keep out of her way. The Cat, deprived of her food, grew leaner and leaner, and finally starved to death. As for Rambé and Ambé, they were accorded a vote of thanks by all their fellow Mice for their wisdom in tricking the evil cat's plan.

125

THE BARUNDA BIRD

A story, a story! Let it go, let it come! You shall hear the sad fate of the Barunda Bird.

The Barunda Bird was a very strange bird indeed, for it had two heads to its body. It is no use looking for such a bird now, for it never existed before, and has never existed since. It had two beaks and two pairs of eyes, and two long necks. Its feathers were green and red, and it lived on berries that grew on bushes in the forest where it made its home. Because of its two heads, the Barunda Bird was really like two birds rolled into one. One head would speak, and the other would reply, and it used to hold conversations with itself all day long.

At first, the Barunda Bird was happy and contented. Of course, one head had to go wherever the other one went, but there was no difficulty about this, because the two heads never argued or quarreled with each other. If the first head were to say, "Let us go this way today," the second head always agreed. If the second head were to say, "Let us make our nest in that tree," the first head would be sure to consent. And they would sing most delightfully, in perfect harmony with one another.

One day, however, as the Barunda Bird was gathering food in the forest, a Snake slithered up beside it. And while the second head was busy pecking berries off

a bush, the Snake spoke to the first head.

"Why do you always agree to do whatever your other head suggests?" hissed the Snake. "He leads you everywhere, and you follow without a word of protest."

The first head listened to the Snake's words, and thought about them as it stretched out its long neck and began to peck more berries from the bush. Meanwhile, the Snake slithered round to the second head, and said:

"How foolish you are to allow yourself to be bullied by that other head of yours! Why don't you think for yourself for a change, and do something on your own account?"

And then, having sown the seeds of discontent, the Snake slithered away through the grass.

From that moment, things changed. The Barunda Bird was no longer happy and contented. Its two heads no longer sang in harmony. It became a miserable, mournful bird, and its green and red feathers drooped and molted as the two heads brooded over the Snake's insinuations.

Now, if one head were to say, "Let us go *this* way today," the other was sure to retort snappishly, "Why should we? No, let us go *that* way instead!" They spent the whole time in argument, and the forest was filled with the shrill sound of their quarreling.

One day, after a particularly bad disagreement, the Barunda Bird was moping miserably along the forest path when the first head suddenly spied a plant that grew

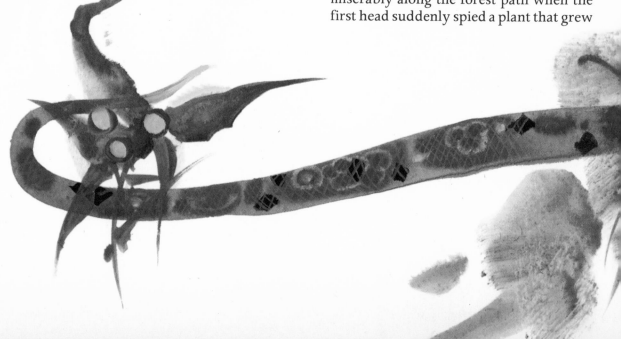

poisonous berries. At once a wicked plan entered its mind.

"If I can persuade that stupid fellow next to me to eat those berries, he will die, and I shall be rid of him for good!" it thought.

So it turned to the second head and said in a cheerful voice: "Look at those tasty yellow berries over there! You eat them first; I will wait until you have had your fill."

The second head was very grateful when it heard this friendly speech. It was just like old times. "It's good of you to suggest it!" it replied.

And it began to peck the poisonous yellow berries with its beak. Alas! As soon as it swallowed them, it began to grimace and roll its eyes, and in a few moments it hung lifeless on its drooping neck.

The first head was delighted with the success of its plan. "That's the end of all my problems!" it thought. "From now on, I shall be able to do whatever I please without having to consult anyone else."

But what was this? Suddenly the first head felt the most terrible pain in its inside. You see, it had quite forgotten that it shared the same stomach as the second head! Too late it repented of its wicked deed; in a very short while it too drooped lifeless. The Barunda Bird was dead.

Oh foolish Barunda Bird, to listen to the insinuations of the slithery Snake! Two people who share the same interest should never allow a third person to divide them.

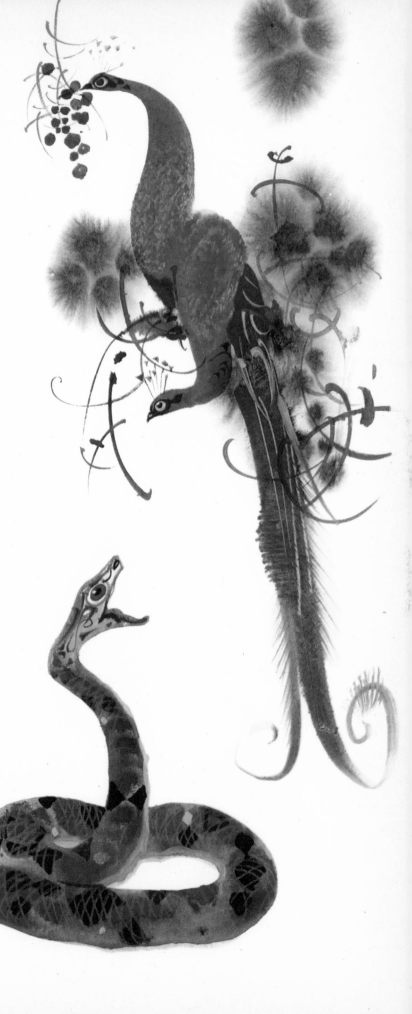

CAT AND MOUSE

Once upon a time a Cat and a Mouse became friends. The Mouse was a church mouse, and used to nest in a broken hassock. The Cat, however, persuaded her to come and live with her. "I have such an affectionate nature that I cannot bear to be parted from you," she told the Mouse.

Well, the Mouse agreed to live with the Cat, and they set up house together. It was then the summer time, but the Cat, shrewd housekeeper as she was, said: "We must make provisions for the winter if we are not to starve from hunger."

The Mouse agreed, and so they bought a pot of fat.

"Where shall we keep it?" asked the Mouse. "We have no larder."

"I know a good place," answered the Cat. "Let us keep it in the church, in a cool dark corner. It will be quite safe there, and when winter comes we can go and fetch it."

They did as the Cat suggested. The days went by, and somehow the Cat could not help thinking longingly of that pot of fat. How she wished she might lick a little off the top! One morning she said to her dear friend the Mouse:

"My cousin has asked me to be godmother at the christening of her little son. I must go to the church today, so you will have to stay here to look after the house."

The Mouse did not suspect that this was a tale made up by the Cat. "Do go, by all means," she said. "And I hope you enjoy the christening."

The Cat set off for the church. But of course there was no cousin, and no kitten to be christened. The Cat stole to the cool dark corner where the pot of fat was hidden, and began to lick off the top. How delicious it was! How she purred with pleasure!

When she came home again, the Mouse asked: "How did the christening go? I hope you had a good day."

"All went according to plan," answered the Cat.

"What name did they give the kitten?" inquired the Mouse.

"Top-off," replied the Cat coolly. "He is snow-white, a lovely child."

"Top-off!" exclaimed the Mouse. "That's a strange name to be sure."

"It is no stranger than 'Crumb-stealer', as one of your godchildren was called," retorted the Cat.

Quite soon after this the Cat was seized again by a great longing to taste some more of the fat. She said to the Mouse: "I am summoned to be godmother at another christening. I must leave you to look after the house once more."

"Don't worry, I shall be all right by myself," replied the Mouse. "I hope you enjoy this christening as much as the last one."

Off went the Cat to the church. She stole to the pot of fat a second time, and found busy work for her long pink tongue. The fat tasted even more delicious than before. She licked her whiskers with enjoyment.

Then she went home.

"I hope you had a good time," the Mouse greeted her. "And what name did they give this kitten?"

"Half-done," answered the Cat in a casual tone of voice. "He is a tortoise shell, a beautiful child."

"Half-done? That is an even stranger name than Top-off!"

"No worse than 'Cheese-nibbler', as I seem to remember another of your godchildren was called," the Cat replied.

It was not long before the Cat's mouth began to water for some more of that delicious fat.

"What do you think?" she said to the Mouse. "I am asked to be godmother a third time. I shall have to go to the church once again while you stay behind at home as before."

Now the Mouse looked thoughtful. "I wonder what name they will give this child?" she said. "Top-off . . . Half-done . . . such odd names, to be sure! But off you go, dear friend – and I really hope everything goes off as well as it has done all the times before!"

The Cat came to the church a third time. She went to the pot of fat in the cool dark corner, and greedily finished up all it

contained. How good it was! She licked round the empty pot, just to make sure she had missed nothing.

"And what did they call this child?" the Mouse asked her when she came home.

"I am afraid you will think this name the most peculiar of all," answered the Cat. "He is called 'All-gone'. Oh he is a remarkable kitten – black with white paws."

"All-gone!" echoed the Mouse. "That name is highly suspicious."

And she looked even more thoughtful than before.

The rest of the summer and the autumn passed peacefully. Strange to say, the Cat was not bidden to any more christenings. Then it was winter. Snow lay on the ground, frost covered the windowpanes, and food was difficult to find. The two friends were hungry. Then the Mouse thought of the wise provision they had made for this time, of the pot of fat hidden in the church.

"Let us go and enjoy the pot of fat we stored up for ourselves," she said to the Cat.

The Cat gave the Mouse a sidelong glance. "Yes, let us do that, dear friend," she agreed.

When they got to the church, the Mouse scampered eagerly to the pot of fat. Imagine her disappointment when she found it had been licked clean!

"Alas!" she squeaked, "now I know that my suspicions were well-founded. You were never bidden to any christenings! You came to the church three times to eat up all the fat. The first time you took the top off, the second time it was half-done, and the third time it was . . ."

"Be quiet!" cried the Cat. "If you say one word more I will eat you, too!"

But "all-gone" was already on the tip of the Mouse's tongue. It passed her lips . . . and immediately the Cat sprang upon her and ate her. And that is the end of the story.

THE BEST WAY TO EAT MONKEY

Listen carefully to this story, for it tells of things that never happened. Old Uncle Wolf was gray and grizzled. He was lazy and greedy, too, and ate everything in sight. His Nephew was young and agile. He worked hard. One fine day, Uncle Wolf said to his Nephew: "Let us each plant a field of manioc."

"That is a good idea," replied his Nephew. "Let us set to work at once."

But that was not Uncle Wolf's idea at all. He sat in the shade and dozed while his Nephew dug the soil and planted two patches of manioc. "Why should I do anything?" thought Uncle Wolf. "My Nephew is young and strong. Let him do all the work!"

The sun shone, the rain fell, and soon the manioc plants put forth green shoots. As soon as Uncle Wolf saw the young shoots showing above the soil in his patch, he went and ate them all up. How good they tasted, how succulent and tender they were!

"I enjoyed those," Uncle Wolf said to himself, smacking his lips. "But I could do with twice that number." And he cast a covetous gaze upon the green shoots growing in his Nephew's patch of manioc. He went up to his Nephew and said: "Show respect to your elders and betters. Give me some of your manioc to eat, for I am very hungry."

"No, Uncle," his Nephew replied. "The plants are not yet ready to eat. They must first grow tall and strong."

Uncle Wolf was angry when he heard this reply. He flew into a rage and chased his Nephew right out of the manioc field. Then he pulled up all the shoots out of his Nephew's patch, and made a good meal of them.

The young Wolf was determined to get his revenge on his greedy Uncle, and so he devised a cunning plan. He went into the forest and cut some strong strands of jute,

and these he braided together to make two strong ropes. Then he went to visit his Uncle.

"So you've come back, have you?" his Uncle greeted him. "I hope you've learned your lesson. You should always show respect to your elders and betters – especially when they are hungry!"

The young Wolf smiled artfully. "Oh, I've forgotten all about the little disagreement we had, Uncle," he replied. "There is something much more serious to worry about. Haven't you heard about the storm?"

"What storm?" growled Uncle Wolf.

His Nephew pointed to the sky. "Do you see that great black cloud in the north?"

"I see it," Uncle Wolf replied. "What of it?"

"In that cloud there is a mighty storm that is coming this way. It will sweep everything before it, and we shall all perish."

Uncle Wolf was very alarmed when he heard this. "Is there no way we can save ourselves?" he asked.

"There is one way," the young Wolf told him. "If we tie ourselves firmly to a tree with a strong rope, we will survive the storm. As a matter of fact, I have just finished making some strong jute rope." And he showed his Uncle the two lengths of rope that he was carrying.

"Oh please, dear Nephew, let me have one of your ropes!" his Uncle begged him.

"Very well, Uncle," his Nephew agreed.

"Now tie me fast to that stout fig tree over there," pleaded the old Wolf. "And see that you make the knots very tight in the rope."

"I will do that for you, Uncle," said his Nephew, smiling to himself. He took one of his strong ropes and bound the old Wolf to the fig tree so tightly that he could not move an inch.

Suddenly, the young Wolf burst out laughing. "There is no storm coming, Uncle!" he cried. "I have played this trick on you to pay you back for stealing my manioc shoots. And now you will have to get someone else to untie you again, for I have business else-

where!'' And still laughing, he ran off.

Uncle Wolf was beside himself with rage when he realized how neatly he had been tricked. Snarling with fury, he strained against the ropes that bound him to the tree, but it was no use: that rascal of a Nephew had seen to it that the knots were tied very tightly, indeed.

The long, hot day went by. Uncle Wolf grew hungry and thirsty. And oh, how stiff he was! Suddenly he heard a noise in the branches above his head. He twisted his neck round as far as he was able, and saw a bright-eyed Monkey squatting among the leaves, eating his fill of ripe, juicy figs.

Uncle Wolf's mouth watered. ''Throw me a fig, friend Monkey! You have no idea how hungry I am!'' he called in a weak voice.

Monkey threw down a fig, and it landed right inside Uncle Wolf's wide-open mouth.

Then Uncle Wolf said: ''You see what a terrible fix I am in, friend Monkey. It is all the fault of my wicked Nephew. Please, I beg of you, be so good as to untie the rope that binds me to this tree.''

But Monkey shook his head. ''You are not a person to be trusted, Uncle Wolf. I know you of old. You have cruel yellow teeth, and could easily devour a small creature like me. I will not release you from the tree just for you to eat me.''

''How can you be so unkind, Monkey? Indeed, I promise faithfully to do you no harm if you will only untie me! I will give you anything you ask for as a reward.''

Monkey again refused to help him, but

the old Wolf went on pleading with him so hard that at last Monkey relented, jumped out of the tree, and undid the knots in the rope. No sooner had the last bond fallen away from Uncle Wolf than he turned on the Monkey and seized him in his cruel yellow teeth.

''Now I am going to eat you up, friend Monkey!'' he snarled.

''Please let me go,'' gibbered the Monkey. ''Remember your promise to me just a minute ago!''

But promises meant nothing to Uncle Wolf. He was hungry, and he was going to eat Monkey.

At that very moment, who should come by but the young Wolf. He had decided it was time to set his Uncle free. He saw what was happening, and realized that he would have to be very quick and clever to save the monkey. He thought for a second or two, then called out:

''Hey, Uncle! Do you know the best way to eat Monkey? Throw him straight up into the air, as hard as you can. He will fall right down into your mouth, and you'll find he will taste delicious that way.''

Uncle Wolf was grateful to his Nephew for this advice. ''Thank you, dear Nephew,'' he said. ''That little tip makes up for the trouble you have caused me so many times in the past.''

And he threw Monkey with all his might straight up in the air. Monkey sailed right back into the leafy branches of the fig tree, and made his escape as fast as he could! Uncle Wolf did not realize what had happened, but stayed there all night with his mouth wide open, waiting for Monkey to fall down again. For all I know, he is waiting there still!

THE SHREWD CICADA

All summer long a Cicada sang in a tall tree. Although he was quite a small insect, he had a loud, shrill voice. Sometimes he spread his transparent wings and flitted from one branch to another, eating the shooting buds and the sweet green leaves.

But although cicadas are content to eat leaves and buds, foxes are not. In fact, a nice, fat, juicy cicada makes a tasty mouthful for a hungry fox!

One day, as the Cicada was chirping merrily in his tree, a prowling Vixen stopped to listen to him. Her mouth watered as she thought of what a succulent tidbit he would make.

"How beautifully you sing!" she called up to the Cicada. "I have heard your song all summer, and now I have come to tell you how much I enjoy listening to it. It is so melodious, so musical! I could never tire of hearing it."

The Cicada looked down at the Vixen.

"The Nightingale and the Lark and the cooing Dove sing more beautifully than I do," he chirped in reply. "I know that. All I do is to make a noise."

The Vixen disagreed. "Oh no, you are quite mistaken. I would much rather listen to your song than the tiresome warblings of the Nightingale or the Lark, or the monotonous cooing of the Dove."

The Vixen's flattery was making the Cicada very suspicious. He peered down at her distrustfully through the leaves.

"However," the Vixen continued, "there is one thing I cannot believe. Everyone tells me you are a very small creature, even smaller than a mouse or a bat. Surely this cannot be true! Your lovely voice is so loud and clear that I feel sure you must be much bigger than that. Come down here beside me, so that I can see for myself what size you are."

But this was one time when the Fox's cunning failed. The Cicada was too wise. He

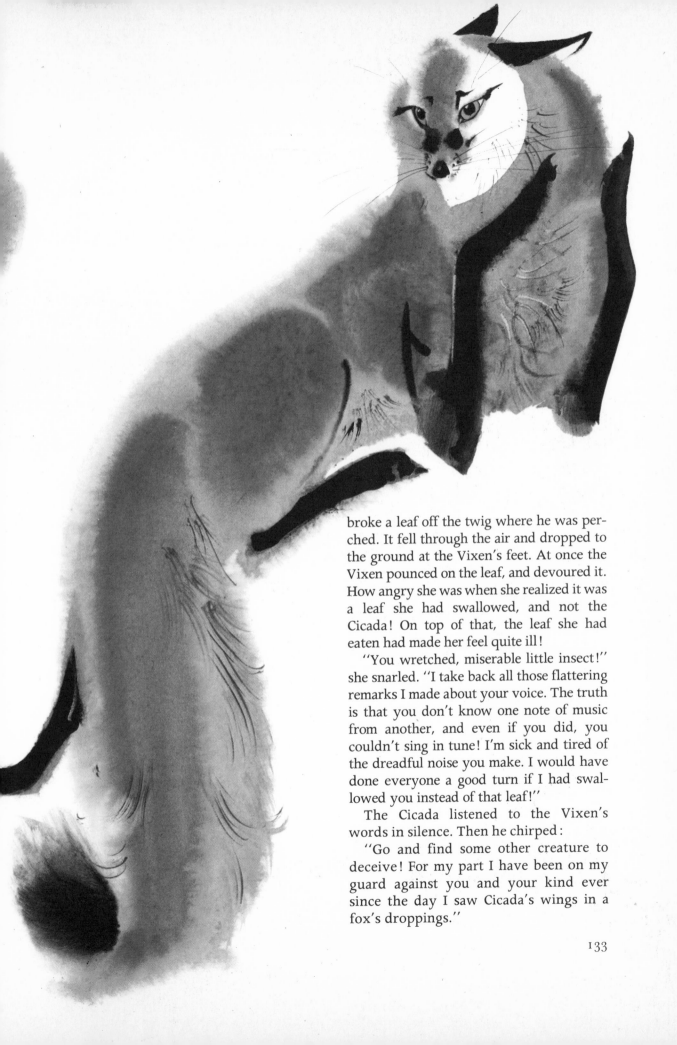

broke a leaf off the twig where he was perched. It fell through the air and dropped to the ground at the Vixen's feet. At once the Vixen pounced on the leaf, and devoured it. How angry she was when she realized it was a leaf she had swallowed, and not the Cicada! On top of that, the leaf she had eaten had made her feel quite ill!

"You wretched, miserable little insect!" she snarled. "I take back all those flattering remarks I made about your voice. The truth is that you don't know one note of music from another, and even if you did, you couldn't sing in tune! I'm sick and tired of the dreadful noise you make. I would have done everyone a good turn if I had swallowed you instead of that leaf!"

The Cicada listened to the Vixen's words in silence. Then he chirped:

"Go and find some other creature to deceive! For my part I have been on my guard against you and your kind ever since the day I saw Cicada's wings in a fox's droppings."

THE JACKAL AND
THE LION

King Lion had ruled the forest for as long as any of the animals could remember. Every creature feared him and ran away in terror at his approach. One day, King Lion called all the animals together and said: "I know what terror I spread among you when I go hunting. Yet I kill only one animal a day for food. Let us come to some better arrangement. If you will provide me with one of your number each day, I will no longer need to hunt for my food. And you will no longer fear me as I roam through the forest."

The animals discussed the King's proposal, and decided it was a good idea. So they agreed that lots should be drawn each evening, and the creature on whom the lot fell should present himself before the Lion at sunrise the next day.

At first, all went according to plan. When the Lion left his den, he strolled harmlessly through the forest, and the other animals no longer fled in terror at his approach. And each sunrise, one of

their number went to the Lion's den to be eaten.

One evening, however, the lot fell on the cunning Jackal. Now the Jackal did not like the thought of being eaten by King Lion at all.

"Why should I provide the Lion's breakfast?" he thought to himself. "It would be better if I could devise a plan to rid the forest of this tyrant once and for all."

And all that night the Jackal thought and thought how this might be achieved.

The next day the Lion woke at sunrise. He looked outside his den, but this morning there was no animal waiting to be eaten! King Lion roared angrily, for he was hungry.

"I'll go and tell those animals what I think of them!" he said. "How dare they forget to send me my breakfast?"

At that moment, however, the Jackal came running through the trees, very much out of breath.

"It's about time you showed up!" roared the Lion. "Why are you so late?"

"Oh, sire," said the Jackal, "please don't be angry. This is what happened. As I was on my way here, I met another Lion who wanted to devour me. But I told him I was on my way to be eaten by you, the King of the Forest. He became very angry when he heard this. He said you were a usurper, and that he was the rightful King of the Forest."

The Lion growled with fury at these words. "Take me to that liar and villain!" he commanded. "I'll soon show him who is the rightful King of the Forest!"

Forthwith, the Jackal led the Lion to a deep well.

"Look down there, sire," he said, pointing to the well. "That is his den."

The Lion peered over the edge of the well. What did he see but another Lion looking up at him! Not realizing it was his own reflection in the water, he sprang into the well with a roar of anger, and was drowned. And that was how the cunning Jackal rid the forest of its tyrant.

135

THE CAT AND THE
RAT

The Cat and the Rat were once great friends, though they have long since forgotten their friendship. You shall hear how they fell out. Many long years ago, they lived together on a little island in the middle of the sea. They led a happy life on the island. The Cat used to catch bright-feathered birds that lived in the trees, and the Rat ate nuts and roots. But no one is ever content with what he has. One day the Rat said to the Cat:

"I am tired of living here on this island. Let us go across the sea to the mainland. There we may find plenty to eat without having to catch birds or dig in the ground for roots."

"That is an excellent idea, dear friend," said the Cat to the Rat. "But how shall we get across the sea to the mainland?"

"That will be quite easy," replied the Rat. "We must make a boat out of a tree root."

So they dug up a huge tree root and began to fashion a boat out of it. The Rat gnawed at the root with his sharp teeth, until he had made a hollow large enough to hold the two of them. The Cat scratched at it with her sharp claws until she had made the outside of the boat quite smooth. Then they found two sticks to serve as paddles, and they set off on their great adventure. Before long they lost sight of the island they had left behind them; yet there was no sign of the mainland.

"Oh dear, oh dear, I am afraid it is much farther across the sea than we thought!" cried the Cat.

"I fear our voyage will take much longer than we imagined!" agreed the Rat in a sad voice.

Now they had foolishly forgotten to take any food with them in the boat. Presently the Cat began to mew plaintively.

"Caungu! Caungu!" she cried, "I'm hungry! I'm hungry!"

The Rat too, began to complain. "Quee! Quee!" he squeaked. "How hungry I am! How hungry I am!"

But there was nothing to be done about it, and so at last the Cat curled herself in a ball and fell asleep. And she dreamed of

the bright-feathered birds she used to catch during the happy days on the island.

The Rat copied the Cat's example, and curled up at the other end of the boat. But he could not sleep. He thought about the tasty nuts and delicious roots he used to eat. And suddenly he remembered that the boat itself was made out of one of those roots!

"I need stay hungry no longer!" he thought to himself; and immediately he began to gnaw at the boat, making the hollow a little deeper. The noise of his sharp teeth against the wood soon woke the Cat.

"What is that noise?" she exclaimed.

But the Rat shut his eyes and pretended to be fast asleep.

"Humph – I must have only imagined I heard a noise," thought the Cat; and she laid her head on her paws and went to sleep once more.

Cautiously the Rat began to eat again – nibble, nibble, nibble!

"I'm *sure* I heard a noise!" cried the Cat, waking up a second time.

She looked across at the Rat, but he still seemed to be fast asleep.

"Humph – I must only have dreamed I heard a noise," the Cat told herself; and she lay down again, with one paw across her eyes.

A third time the Rat began to gnaw at the root – nibble, nibble, nibble. But this time he gnawed a hole right through the bottom of the boat, and the water began to come in.

"Oh! What has. happened now!" shrieked the Cat, jumping up and balancing herself on the side of the boat. She did not like the water at all. She glared across at the Rat. "You did this! You gnawed a hole in the boat with your sharp teeth!" she accused him angrily.

"I did not mean to gnaw a hole," protested the Rat. "I only meant to take a little snack because I was so hungry!"

At that moment, the boat began to sink, and the Cat and the Rat were forced to take to the water and swim for their lives. By now, however, they were within sight of the mainland.

"Just you wait till we get ashore," hissed the Cat as they swam. "I am going to eat you up! A fine friend you have proved yourself!"

"I deserve it," squeaked the Rat.

At last they reached the shore and stood on dry land once more.

"And now," said the Cat to the Rat, "I hope you are ready to provide a meal for me."

"Yes, yes, certainly!" squeaked the Rat. "But don't you think it would be better to wait until I dry myself? Otherwise, the taste of sea-water will spoil your meal. Just wait until I am quite dry."

"Very well," agreed the Cat.

So they sat down under a tree and dried their coats in the sun. The Cat was a vain creature. She was so intent upon licking her coat smooth and glossy that she did not notice what the Rat was doing. He was busily digging a hole in the ground.

At last the Cat had licked every hair of her coat into place. "Are you ready?" she asked the Rat.

"I'm ready!" the Rat replied – and quick as a flash he disappeared into the hole.

The Cat was very angry indeed.

"Quee! Quee!" called the Rat from the bottom of the hole.

"You need not think you are so clever, my friend," the Cat told him. "I shall simply stay here and wait until you come out."

"What if I don't come out?" said the Rat.

"Then you will stay there and starve," said the Cat.

And she crouched down beside the entrance to the hole, with all four feet tucked under her, resting her nose on her paws.

All day long the Rat went on digging in the earth.

All day long the Cat watched and waited beside the hole.

By the time darkness fell, the Rat had dug his way right under the ground to the other side of the tree. He crept out of the far end of his tunnel and made his escape. And still the Cat stayed at her end of the hole. For all I know, she is waiting there still!

THE MOUSE KEEPS
HER PROMISE

In the heat of the noonday sun a Lion lay sleeping, his great tawny body stretched out on the ground. Suddenly he felt something running up his belly, along his back, over his head, and down his nose, and with a roar he woke up. There before his eyes, petrified by the sound of the Lion's displeasure, was a little Mouse. She quivered with fright, from the tip of her twitching pink nose to the tip of her twitching pink tail. The Lion stretched out one paw and seized the Mouse in his powerful grasp.

"So you are the creature that dares to disturb me while I am asleep!" he growled.

"Oh, please, Lord Lion, I did not mean to disturb you!" squeaked the Mouse. "I mistook your body for a great mountain that I must climb over. Please forgive me!"

The Lion held the Mouse an inch from his nose. "I don't know that I shall forgive you," he said sulkily. "I was having such a pleasant nap, and now you've spoiled it." Then he added slowly: "I think I am going to eat you."

"Oh, don't do that, Lord Lion, please don't do that! I would make a miserable mouthful for a great creature such as you! I would not provide a satisfying meal at all."

"I don't want a satisfying meal," the Lion replied. "I just feel like a snack. A mouthful of mouse would fill the little empty space in my belly very well."

The Mouse was desperate. How could she escape the Lion's jaws?

"I will make a bargain with you, Lord Lion," she said. "If you spare my life and let me go free, I will come to your help if ever you are in danger."

This speech amused the Lion. He laughed so much that tears came to his eyes.

"How could you, such an insignificant little creature as you are, help me if ever I ran into danger?" he scoffed. "However, you have succeeded in putting me into a good humor, and I will let you go after all."

And he opened his paw and let the Mouse out of his grasp.

"Never fear, Lord Lion, I shan't forget my half of the bargain!" she squeaked as she scurried away.

Not long after this, the Lion was chased by hunters. Try as he might, he could not escape them. They chased him across the plains and into the forest, and at last they caught him. They passed a strong rope around his body and tied him to a tree. Then they went off to find other sport.

"We shall come back presently to finish you off!" they promised the Lion.

The Lion roared with rage and growled with despair. He jerked his body this way and that, but he could not struggle free. The rope held him fast.

Far away in the forest, the little Mouse heard the Lion's roars.

"The Lion is in danger!" she thought. "I must go to help him as I promised."

She ran as fast as she could until she reached the place where the Lion was held captive.

"Here I am, Lord Lion! I have come to help you, according to our bargain," she squeaked.

And without more ado she set to work with her sharp little teeth, and bit through every strand of the strong rope that held the Lion to the tree. The rope fell apart; the Lion was free.

"You laughed at me the other day, Lord Lion," said the Mouse. "You never imagined I would be able to repay your kindness in sparing my life. But now you see that even an insignificant little creature such as myself may help a Lion out of danger!"